THE MODEEN FACTOR

FRANK H JORDAN

ACKNOWLEDGMENTS

These books are written in Australian English.

The situations, organisations and characters in these books are fictional, and any resemblance to an existing or past entity is entirely coincidental.

With thanks to Genista Fereselle for French language services.

DEDICATION

To returned Australian service men and women - you are appreciated more than you know.

THE AUTHOR

A long time fan of Lee Child's Jack Reacher novels and Matthew Reilly's fast-paced stories, ex-Army Reservist and Queensland author Frank H Jordan penned his own high-action series, inspired by the brave men and women of the Australian Defence Force.

Enter, ex-SASR soldier Jo Modeen.

The Modeen Factor is the first book in the high-action JO MODEEN series, followed by a growing number of thrilling instalments featuring the gutsy heroine.

Decorated soldier Josephine Dakota Modeen, the first woman to be accepted into Australia's elite SASR, finds life after the Army unfulfilling.
When contacted out of the blue by her old CO, she knows it's not a social call. Hearing from Ben Logan VC means a mission, no exceptions....

CHAPTER ONE

At the mission briefing they were given the settlement's coordinates, not its name. Murmuring to Wolf, 'Not a need to know, I guess,' she received a grunt in reply.

Later, as they left the briefing, he threw her a half-smart glance and drawled, 'You bringin' Walt on this one, Modeen?'

'Always.' She patted the Walther PPX concealed beneath her jacket. 'Someone's gotta keep Gator safe, he still owes me twenty bucks.'

Trooper Jo Modeen rested the muzzle of her assault rifle, an H and K MP5SD6, on top of the sand-covered stone wall. The Special Forces squad had been kitted out with the silenced version of the MP5 before being dropped near the outskirts of a derelict village on the edge of the desert. Their assignment – to neutralise the armed insurgents entrenched in an old stone dwelling and causing trouble for advancing troops.

From her position behind the wall, Modeen covered the backs of squad members Ben, Wolf and Gator as they entered the rear of the crumbling building some twenty metres away. She waited the prescribed thirty seconds and was about to emerge when three guerrillas, armed with AK47s, appeared around the side of the dwelling. Ducking back behind cover, she risked a peek over the wall and saw the guerrillas saunter to the rear entrance, weapons slung over their shoulders. After a brief pause by the doorway, they vanished inside.

Cursing through tight lips, she ran through the scenario in her head.

Close quarters and stealth.

Slinging the MP5 over a shoulder, she sprang to her feet and, keeping low, raced toward the building. Yanking the PPX from beneath her vest as she ran, she pulled back and released the slide and heard the reassuring sound of the first round slamming into the chamber. She was five metres from the entrance when another guerrilla appeared around the corner to her right. He propped on seeing her and then slumped to his knees, before falling face-first into the sand with a neat entry hole in his forehead.

Keeping 'Walt' at the ready, Modeen slid to a stop beside the building's rear entrance. With her back pressed hard against the wall, she peered around the doorway's splintered timber frame. The dwelling's interior was almost as rough as its exterior. There were no internal doors, and the floors were bare, compacted earth beneath bullet-ridden walls. After a hasty glance around to check for more advancing guerrillas, she pushed off the wall and strode with purpose into the first room, scanning left to right and holding Walt ahead of her, finger poised on the trigger.

As expected, the room was empty.

Clear.

She moved into the next room, once again checking left to right.

Clear.

As she entered the third, the hair on the back of her neck stood on end. Her PPX hissed and flashed twice in the dimly lit room, dropping two of the insurgents to her right. Before she could engage the third on her left, Wolf had spun around and strafed the man with two short bursts from his MP5. As he slammed against the wall, the rebel let out a scream and slid to the floor, releasing a spray of bullets into the already cracked ceiling.

Lowering her head so the dislodged rubble and dust fell on her combat helmet, Modeen sighed as all hell broke loose inside the dwelling.

So much for stealth.

From the commotion, she estimated there were at least ten insurgents in the fourth, front room. Ben was backed against the wall near the doorway with his MP5 in his left hand. At the sound of advancing feet, he yanked the bayonet from its scabbard and in one fluid movement, drove the seven inch blade deep into the throat of the first rebel to rush into the room. Gurgling, the man fell backward, momentarily blocking the doorway.

At a nod from Ben, Gator yanked two grenades from his vest, pulled the pins and rolled them into the front room.

With urgent hand signals to his squad members, Ben laid down suppressing fire as all four raced out of the building. They had just cleared the rear exit when the front room exploded. Keeping their heads down, they sprinted across the heavy sand toward the wall. Modeen reached it first and wasted no time in turning and raising her MP5 to cover their retreat.

When an insurgent appeared in the building's doorway and aimed his rifle at them, she let loose a single shot … just as Gator unknowingly ducked into her line of fire. He gave a yell as the bullet grazed his shoulder making him jerk violently sideways. Behind him, the insurgent's weapon slipped from his hands as he dropped to his knees and then toppled face-first to the ground.

Clenching his teeth, Gator regained his balance and ran to the safety of the wall. Once behind it he fell to his knees clutching his shoulder, swearing under his breath and glaring at Modeen. She merely shrugged and maintained her watch as Wolf dug out a dressing and applied it to Gator's bleeding shoulder.

They stayed hunkered down there, silently waiting and watching for stragglers, until Ben declared it safe for them to proceed to the evac point.

———

To Josephine Modeen, that final tour of duty felt like a long time ago and a world away as she cruised along the Princess Motorway on a typical Australian morning. Under a cloudless expanse of sky, she sat at ease and comfortable behind the protective faring of her GTR 1400cc motorcycle.

The bike suited her lifestyle. A single woman, she travelled light. In contrast, she 'lived heavy' by her own standards, although the small penthouse apartment on the Gold Coast wasn't of her choosing. It had been an unsolicited gift, intended to provide a civilian base where she could live a 'normal' life … or so they said when insisting she accept it. But she knew what it was, this generous gift. It was one of the so-called perks of being an only child of wealthy, controlling parents.

High court magistrate John Modeen and wife Freda, the daughter of a wealthy South African plantation owner, had emigrated to Australia in the early 1970s to settle in Sydney. When their defiantly tomboyish daughter announced her intention to enlist in the Australian Army, the well-to-do couple was none too pleased, to say the least.

Her father had glared at her from his impressive height, making her feel like a child again. 'And just *what* do you intend to do,' he demanded in his best magistrate's voice, 'once you've finished dancing to the erratic tugs of the puppet master's strings?'

Not waiting for her to answer, he'd raised a hand to announce loftily, 'You'll soon become disillusioned with political capriciousness, or you're no daughter of mine. And what sort of civilian job will soldiering qualify you for, hmm? A pig shooter? A snoring security guard?' He tugged on his lapels and stuck out his chest. 'Now as a lawyer, you'd have the justice system's upper echelon to aspire to. But what career path does military service offer? Do you hope to rise through the ranks?' Staring down his nose at her, he gave a disdainful sniff. 'How many female Army generals do *you* know?'

Through the tinted visor of her full-face helmet, Modeen read *Lawrence Hargrave Drive Exit 500 metres* on a fast-approaching green highway sign. The bike gave a smooth growl and surged forward as she accelerated to change lanes. Taking the exit ramp, she abandoned the busy motorway in favour of the scenic route that snaked along the ocean. Glancing every now and then at the passing vista, she crossed Sea Cliff Bridge and motored through Scarborough.

Returning to her previous train of thought she sighed, recalling her naive assumption that being successful in her chosen occupation would change her parents' attitudes toward it. But instead of easing into resigned tolerance, their resentment, her father's in particular, had only intensified with each of her achievements. While her mother had secretly congratulated her on being selected as the first female to try out for, and be accepted into, the elite Special Air Services Regiment, her father had chosen to disparage the hard-won distinction as he did all her military awards.

She clicked her tongue. The strained relationship with her father was like a burr under her blanket.

And now I've had time to wind down from active service, time to think about my future, I actually AM wondering what there is for an ex-Special Forces soldier to do that's worthwhile, satisfying, and mentally stimulating. I 'spose I could re-train and become an accountant, or a legal secretary … or maybe a barista?

A wry grin tugged at the corners of her mouth as, keeping to the coast, she followed Memorial Drive south. It would take her through Wollongong and on to Batemans Bay, where she'd booked into the Esplanade Hotel for the night.

As the bike ate up the miles, her thoughts turned to the reason for the road trip, and the invitation that was more like an order from her old CO, Ben Logan. On leaving the force almost two years ago, she'd followed tradition and promised to stay in touch with her SASR mates, but life, as it has a habit of doing, had put distance between them.

That was why it came as a surprise when, out of the blue, Ben had called....

'JD, I need you to come to a wedding.'

'Is that you, Ben?'

'It's next Saturday, in Melbourne. I've arranged for you to stay with Jen Walters, one of the bridesmaids.'

'Nice to hear from you too, Ben. Still got no time for small talk I see.'

'Jen's expecting you to arrive on the Friday at her place on Toorak Road West – said you're welcome to stay the week if you like. She thinks you're just a friend of the family attending the wedding.'

'O ... kay.' Modeen knew it wasn't a social call. Her old CO didn't 'do' social calls, at least not to his old squad members. 'So what's the mission?'

Ben gave an amused snort and then sobered. 'I need you to do some recon, on the quiet. I have suspicions about Jen's other half.'

'What sort of suspicions?'

'Reckon he might be mistreating her.'

'And if he is, surely that's a matter for the police?'

'*I'll* handle it JD.' His words were clipped, precise, his deep voice unwavering. 'The police can't do much in domestic violence cases, and tickling him with a feather won't cut it. If my suspicions are confirmed, I want his "activities" stopped.'

'Ooh.' She grinned wickedly, 'I'd hate to be in his shoes.'

'You in?'

'You bet.'

'I'll text you the details. See you in Melbourne.'

———

Pulling into the hotel car park, Modeen switched off the GTR's ignition and removed her helmet, raking fingers through her closely cropped platinum-blonde hair and running a hand over her face. Out of habit she fingered the scar on her cheek. It was only a slight indentation, courtesy of a bullet that got close enough to graze her.

The second and last one to get that close.

With a roll of her left shoulder she got off the bike, stretched, and looked around, giving her ears time to adjust after hours of big motor hum. Taking a deep breath of the salty coastal air, she bent to unclip the GTR's roomy panniers containing her gear. Slipping her helmet over her arm, she picked up the two panniers and strode into reception to check in, her snug-fitting black leathers creaking as she walked.

The thought of a warm shower, followed by a cold drink to wash away the highway dust and dinner, was more than inviting. Grateful to find herself the only guest at the desk, she greeted the receptionist and handed over her credit card.

'Modeen, for one night. I'll be making an early start in the morning so I'll settle the account now, thanks.'

An early start … to finish the last eight hour leg of the journey to Melbourne.

When the alarm on her smart phone chimed at just before five am she was already awake. With military precision she showered, dressed, threw the last few things into the panniers, and left the room, soundlessly locking the door behind her. The need for caution and stealth had been ingrained in her, and she had no desire to exorcise the useful skills in her kitbag of talents.

Making her way through the deserted lobby, she deposited the room key in the early departure security box. Once outside in the early morning chill, she fastened the panniers onto the GTR, locking them into place, and pulled her black helmet over her still-damp hair.

The instant she inserted the key and hit the start button, the bike's motor roared into throbbing life and subsided to a throaty purr. Settling herself on the wide, padded seat – long trip comfort was one of the reasons she'd chosen that model – Modeen kicked the GTR into gear, pulled out of the car park, and re-joined the highway.

Two and a half hours later her stomach told her it was time to stop. At the next set of golden arches she pulled in for a late breakfast. After collecting her loaded tray, she headed instinctively for a corner table where she could sit with her back against the wall. From there, she watched the comings and goings of the busy takeaway while she ate.

Seeing a man in camouflage cargoes stroll past her table got her musing on the last mission of her Special Forces unit. She took another bite of her bacon and egg muffin, recalling how Gator had ribbed her about grazing him on purpose. He'd accused her of getting back at him for failing to cough up the twenty bucks he owed her from their last poker game.

Thinking wryly, *and I still haven't seen a cent of that money,* she drained her coffee cup and rose to make her way out to the waiting bike.

CHAPTER TWO

After cruising along Toorak Road West checking house numbers, Modeen nosed the GTR to the curb outside a Victorian-styled terrace house. Sitting on the bike with the engine running, she took in the well-maintained paintwork on the gracious old building, lacy metal fretwork on the upper and lower balconies, and the cottage garden surrounded by a high wrought iron fence.

Certain she was at the right place, she idled the bike into the narrow driveway and parked on a patch of lawn in the front garden. She was dismounting when a slender young woman opened the front door and stepped onto the porch.

'Jo?'

Modeen removed her helmet, smiled and nodded.

The young woman came down the stairs. 'Hi, I'm Jenny.' She made her way along the cobbled path, eyeing the GTR. 'Hey, nice wheels! Ben said you'd probably be on a bike.'

'OK to park it here?'

'Fine.'

Modeen inclined her head toward the terrace house. 'You've got a lovely home.'

'Thanks.' Jenny flicked it a backward glance. 'When we inherited it the place needed a bit of work, but it's been a labour of love.'

As the two women shook hands Jenny winced. 'With a grip like that, you're one of Ben's ex-Army mates alright.'

Hastily releasing her hand, Modeen murmured, 'Sorry.'

Jenny stretched her fingers as she went on. 'But he didn't mention you were so tall, and pretty.' She gave a shy smile. 'How tall *are* you?'

'Five eleven.'

Jenny nodded. 'Right. Well, come on in. Would you like a cup of tea?'

'Thanks Jen, but could you make it a coffee?'

'Sure.'

After unclipping the panniers from the bike, Modeen followed Jenny along the path to the house. 'And I could do with a visit to the little girls' room?'

'Of course.' Jenny held the front door open for her. 'The bathroom's the last door on the left at the end of the hall. Just leave your gear near the stairs. Oh, and how do you like your coffee?'

'White with one, thanks.'

Modeen pulled up a chair at the shabby chic kitchen table and watched as Jenny made their drinks.

'Help yourself to the sugar.' Jenny placed a mug of coffee in front of her. 'So, Ben tells me you're a security guard up in Queensland?'

'Thanks. Yeah, that's right.' Modeen gave an amused snort. 'Ben sure keeps his finger on the pulse.' She blew on her mug and took a thoughtful sip. 'We haven't seen each other since I left the Army two years ago.'

'His knowing stuff is just … Ben being Ben,' Jenny said with a smile, 'or so his sister tells me.' Bringing her cup of tea to the table, she took a seat opposite Modeen and fixed her with a penetrating gaze. 'You must be brave to be a security guard.'

'Most of the time nothing much happens that requires bravery.' Modeen took another sip of her coffee. It was hot and strong, just the way she liked it. 'In security work, you're on your own for hours on end. It can be awfully boring.'

'Right. But if something *did* happen…?'

'I'd deal with it.' Modeen sat back to gaze at Jenny from over the rim of her mug, taking in the paleness of her cheeks and the shadows around her almond-shaped eyes. She shrugged. 'After all, that's what I'm there for.'

'Right, right.' Jenny looked out the window, pensively chewing her bottom lip, while Modeen took another mouthful of coffee. After a bit Jenny turned back, saying, 'So … what does JD stand for?'

'Josephine Dakota. But I prefer Jo or Modeen. That's what most of the guys in the force used to call me. Only Ben calls me JD.' She drained her mug.

'Jo. Right. Now, I guess you'll want to freshen up?' At Modeen's nod in reply, Jenny rose to her feet. 'Okay, I'll show you to your room.'

Modeen collected her gear and followed her host up the polished timber staircase and along a short hallway. They passed what looked to be a sizeable master bedroom and then Jenny opened a door into a smaller, sunlit room.

'You're in here, Jo.'

Modeen took in the tall brass bed, antique wardrobe and dressing table, and the tasteful pictures adorning the pastel-coloured walls. Striding to the lace-curtained window, she looked down into the front garden and out to the busy street.

She turned to Jenny. 'This is really nice.'

'Thanks. I've put a towel in the downstairs bathroom for you. If there's anything else you need, just sing out. Peter won't be home 'til about eight-thirty.'

The crease in Jenny's brow at the mention of her husband's name wasn't lost on Modeen, nor was the unsteadiness of her host's hands. There was something bird-like about the young woman, as though she ran on nervous energy.

'On Fridays he likes to spend a few hours at the pub after work, to unwind.' She gnawed her bottom lip and then realised Modeen was watching. Her expression cleared and she said brightly, 'I figured you'd be hungry after the long trip, so dinner's at six. I've made beef bourguignon.'

'Sounds great. So where does he work, your Peter?'

'At the steel mill. He's a fitter and turner by trade.' A bevy of emotions crossed Jenny's face as she turned to leave, saying over her shoulder, 'Anyway, make yourself at home, Jo.'

Jenny's beef bourguignon was delicious, as was the sticky date pudding that followed it. Savouring her last mouthful, Modeen was silently thanking Ben for arranging such agreeable accommodations when her conscience pricked her with a reminder of why she was there. Chastising herself for being lulled by the pleasant surroundings and good-natured host, she refocused her attention on the purpose of her visit.

After they'd cleared the dishes and stacked the dishwasher, the two women retired to the living room to finish the bottle of wine Jenny had opened with dinner. They'd only just settled into the comfy armchairs when they heard someone staggering up the back stairs.

'That'll be Pete.' Jenny sprang to her feet and went to greet him at the back door.

When she ushered him past the living room and into the kitchen, Modeen rose and moved closer to the doorway, ostensibly to examine the oil painting above the fireplace. But it was her ears, not her eyes, that were on alert … for what transpired in the kitchen. She could hear Jenny fussing over her husband while serving him his meal, and his occasional grunts in response.

When Jenny came back into the room, she found Modeen peering at the photographs on the mantelpiece. In pride of place was a gold-framed picture of a beaming Jenny in bridal garb, standing beside a smug-looking, well-built man Modeen assumed was Peter. Next to it in a more recent picture, Jenny was easily recognisable as the blushing bride of the earlier photo, while a pudgy, balding Peter looked very little like his younger self. The supercilious expression was the same, however, only more blatant.

A shout echoed from the kitchen. 'Haven't we got any beer?'

With a nervous start, Jenny called, 'Coming, Love.' As she made to dash out, Modeen said quietly, 'Look Jen, I've had a big day and feel like an early night. Think I'll turn in. See you both in the morning. And thanks again for a lovely dinner.'

'You're welcome, Jo,' a distracted Jenny threw over her shoulder. 'See you in the morning.'

. . .

After slipping into a pair of soft cotton tracky pants and cropped tee-shirt, Modeen retrieved a Macintosh tablet from one of her panniers and climbed into bed. She was checking her messages when she heard heavy footsteps on the floor below. Sitting still, she listened and heard a distinct thud, followed by the squawk of the TV being turned on.

Focusing her attention back to the tablet, she finished reading her emails. At around twenty-three hundred hours when the house fell silent, she closed the tablet, rolled onto her side, and gave her heavy, travel-weary eyelids permission to close.

At one of their early sorties, Gator had told her with gruff admiration, 'Reckon you sleep with one eye open, Modeen.' He had dared a big-noting private to steal the pack of cards she kept in her boots, while she was sleeping. With the other squad members looking on, the cocky young private had crept over to her swag. Squatting and reaching for her boots, he'd frozen mid-reach when the tip of her knife's blade pressed against his throat.

'Lookin' for something?' she'd enquired coolly, to the great amusement of Gator and the other members of the troop.

Yes, in her line of work, being a light sleeper certainly had its advantages....

. . .

Rising early the next morning, Modeen jogged down Toorak Road toward the Royal Botanic Gardens, admiring the war memorials as she passed. By the time she was heading back to Jenny's on the last leg of her ten kilometre run, the city had come alive with the rattle of trams and other early morning commuter bustle.

Once back in her room, still warm from the run, Modeen finished her morning workout with sit-ups and push-ups, and then took a shower and got dressed. Not long after, she heard Jenny stirring and smelled the aroma of coffee. Stepping out of her room, she eased the door closed behind her and made her way to the kitchen.

Peter didn't surface until ten. The steps creaked under his weight as he made his way downstairs. Shuffling into the kitchen he barked, 'Coffee, Love.'

'Right here.' Jenny put a steaming mug on the table in front of him. 'Would you like another one, Jo?'

'Yes please.' Modeen addressed her response to Jenny but was staring at her husband, sizing him up.

Seeing that, Jenny said in a rush, 'Jo, this is my husband Peter.'

Modeen rose and extended a hand. She and Peter were the same height, but that was where their similarities ended. While she was tall, slim and athletic, he was tall, flabby and unfit.

He took her compact, capable hand in his meaty one. Muttering, 'Not a bad grip,' he sniggered, showing cracked, nicotine-stained teeth. 'Could use you down at the mill, we need another tea lady.'

And there it is, she thought cynically. *Didn't take him long to descend into idiocy.*

Letting it slide, she sat down again as Jenny piped up, 'Jo's a security guard.'

'Really, a female guard?' Peter shot her a doubting look and scoffed, 'Well, I'm sure that's fine if you're up against a gang of smurfs. But what if a real crim fronted up to you, say a man my size?'

Fixing him with a disdainful gaze, she replied evenly, 'Haven't met anyone that couldn't be stopped by a bullet.'

'Oh! So a pretty thing like you plays with guns?'

'They're standard issue for the work I do.'

An apprehensive Jenny interrupted them. 'You should see her motorbike, Pete. It's a beauty.'

'Let me guess,' he sneered, 'a little pink Vespa?'

Unruffled, Modeen eyed him levelly.

I've got your measure, pal.

Jenny's brittle smile dissolved and she threw Modeen an apologetic glance. 'No, it's that big blue one out the front.'

Rising to her feet, Modeen went to the sink and rinsed her mug. 'Don't worry about the second cup for me, Jen, I'm going to hit the shops. What time are we leaving for the wedding?'

'It starts at four, so I'd like us to leave here around

three. Because I'm in the bridal party, I need to be there well before the guests start arriving.'

'No worries, I'll be back in plenty of time.'

For part of the way Modeen retraced the route she had taken earlier that morning, except this time she walked diagonally through the park and across the Yarra river into the bustling inner city. Turning down Bourke Street, she followed the aroma of freshly roasted coffee beans to a quiet, softly-lit café.

As she savoured her barista-brewed flat white, her froth-tipped mouth stretched into a grin. She recalled Ben telling her at the awards ceremony of the battle he'd had with his wife's treasured espresso machine, one from which he hadn't emerged victorious. For a man of few words, he'd been unusually chatty in the lead-up to the award presentations. But when his turn came, and with his jubilant loved ones looking on, he stood tall, broad-shouldered and proud while receiving the prestigious Victoria Cross, the highest award for any member of the Australian Defence Force.

Modeen's own family had declined her invitation to attend the ceremony, despite the fact that she too received an award, the Star of Gallantry for 'heroism in circumstances of great peril'. It was clear that time hadn't dimmed her father's contempt for his daughter's choice of military service as a career. Refusing to let her parents' snub spoil the day, Modeen had instead focused on celebrating Ben's award for efforts 'above and beyond the call of duty' during Operation Slider.

The award presenter had described how, when deployed by helicopter into a nest of enemy machine gunners, Ben and his unit had been pinned down. After they'd managed to neutralise one of the enemy machine guns, Ben dispatched two of the insurgents by hand and exposed his position to draw fire away from the other troops. He then single-handedly stormed two more of the remaining machine gunners, defeating them both at close quarters, while the squad overpowered the third.

Yes, that VC was well deserved.

Modeen smiled at the memory of Ben's muscular six foot four frame towering over everyone else at the gala occasion. But he'd projected only cool composure amidst all the pomp and ceremony.

Just another walk in the park for Corporal Ben Logan….

CHAPTER THREE

After exploring the city and touring the old Melbourne Jail, Modeen found a cosy spot for lunch in an Irish-themed pub. She sat listening to the Irish music issuing from the wall-mounted speakers and watched the other diners chatting, flirting, eating, or growing increasingly wobbly on their bar stools courtesy of copious amounts of Stout.

After lunch, she headed back to the terrace house to find Jenny upstairs, getting ready for the wedding. A dinner-suited Peter was in the lounge room having a beer in front of the TV. Seeing his dour, less than impressed expression, brought on by the tightness of his suit she decided, Modeen skirted the room and skipped upstairs. Grabbing her wedding outfit and toiletries bag from her room, she went back down and headed to the bathroom.

After shedding her clothes, she stepped into the

shower and went to task with the soap and shampoo. At one stage she thought she heard the bathroom door rattle and pulled aside the shower curtain to check, but all was well in the room. All the same, she was glad she'd locked the door out of habit.

Emerging from the bathroom she found Jenny, all made up and gorgeous in a figure-hugging satin gown and with her hair piled in glossy waves on top of her head, doing twirls in front of her husband. When she came to a stop after the last twirl, Modeen glimpsed a bruise on her shoulder. She'd obviously tried to cover it with make-up, but its dark shadow was still visible under the shoestring strap of her gown.

When he noticed Modeen watching from the doorway Peter rose, turned off the TV, and said gruffly, 'I'll get the car out.'

They arrived at the church in good time. When Jenny dashed off to 'do her bridesmaid thing' as Peter put it, Modeen spied Ben stepping out of another car. At her approach, his face lit up and he pulled her into a bear hug.

'Good to see you, JD.'

'You too, Ben.'

Still smiling, he indicated the smartly dressed woman standing behind him. 'You know my wife Emily?'

'Yes of course,' Modeen replied warmly. 'Hi Emily, it's been a while.' The two women greeted each other with a kiss on the cheek.

'Nice to see you, Jo. And would you like to meet our new addition?' Emily moved aside to reveal a pram.

'Oh, wow! Who's this?' Modeen cooed, eyeing the little bundle of joy.

'Chelsea.'

'Well, well.' She leaned over the pram to peer at the tiny sleeping form swaddled in pink. 'You two *have* been busy.'

'And speaking of busy,' Emily said ruefully, 'I think she needs changing. So if you'll excuse me….' She began wheeling the pram away only to turn and throw them a stern glance. 'Now I don't want you two talking shop the whole time. No gory war stories, do I make myself clear?'

Swallowing a grin, Ben saluted and barked, 'Ma'am, yes Ma'am!'

Emily arched an eyebrow at him in mild amusement as she headed toward the amenities, leaving the two of them gazing after her.

'You've got a great family there, Ben.'

'Thanks. I'm a lucky man.'

'So, who's wedding is this anyway?'

'Anne-Marie's.' At Modeen's blank stare, Ben elaborated. 'My little sister's.'

'Oh … right.'

'Didn't I tell you that before?'

Modeen shook her head at him. 'You were a bit stingy with the details.' Narrowing her eyes, she murmured, 'But that's okay, 'cos you're generous with the ones that count.'

During the wedding ceremony, Modeen studied the assembled throng from her position at the back of the church, and found it easy to 'spot the Logan'. Ben's parents were both tall and well built, his sister the same. Modeen smiled, recalling someone describing the Logan family as 'The Karri trees of the human forest'.

She smiled again during the signing of the marriage certificate. At the sight of Anne-Marie's no-nonsense, resolute expression as she signed her maiden name for the last time, Modeen gave a silent snort.

I know that look.

As the happy couple made their way to the beribboned limousine, the guests gathered on either side of the pathway to shower them with rose petals before they were ferried away for photographs. Taking advantage of the commotion, Ben pulled Modeen to one side.

'How's the surveillance going?'

'Peter Walters is an obnoxious, condescending pig,' she replied sweetly while throwing her last handful of petals in the air above the beaming bride, 'but I haven't seen him *physically* hurt her.' She brushed her now empty hands together. 'He strikes me as the type though, and she does have a suspicious-looking bruise on one shoulder.' Pursing her lips, she mused, 'Though she could've got that by simply bumping into something.'

While joining the other guests in waving off the newlyweds, she continued with her report, taking care to keep her voice low. 'Seeing the way she panders to him, I'd say Jenny must have a victim complex. Why else would she put up with his demeaning crap?'

Ben didn't speak or look at her, but she could tell he was listening intently while waving at the departing limo.

'If you like, I'll hang around 'til Tuesday. I've got some old friends I wouldn't mind looking up while I'm here.'

'Thanks JD, appreciate it.'

'Any time, Ben, you know that. But let's face facts. What can you or I do if we discover your suspicions are correct, only to find Jenny won't stand up to him?'

He squinted at her and rapped, 'Leave that to me,' making her feel like she was once more talking to *Corporal* Ben Logan. 'Here, take this.' He handed her a late model Nokia mobile. 'Keep it on you at all times and let me know if anything eventuates. I've put my details in the contact list, and if you get into trouble just hit my number and I'll have someone there ASAP.'

'Hang on, this is a bit over the top isn't it? I have my own phone, why don't you just give me your number?'

'Let's just say I feel safer knowing you have *that* phone.'

'Really? What aren't you telling me?' She gave him a sideways look. 'Should I have brought Walt along?'

'No.' But his eyes glinted. 'You kept the PPX, hey?'

She gave a nonchalant shrug. 'I just like to play it safe and have all my bases covered.'

He gave an amused grunt.

'Tell me something, Ben?'

'Fire away.'

'What made you so sure I'd be able to drop everything and come to this wedding?'

He lowered his head and said softly, 'I've got eyes and ears all over the place these days, JD.'

'Oh yeah?' Her eyes lit up with curiosity. 'So who are you working for now?'

'I—' Taking a quick glance over his shoulder, Ben said hurriedly, 'I'll be in touch before you leave, with a proposition.'

'A proposition? That's interesting.' Leaning in to whisper, 'Why can't you tell me now?' she saw Ben tilt his head toward an approaching Emily.

Marching up to them, she ordered, 'Right you two, break it up. What did I tell you about this?' and she waved an accusing finger from one to the other and back again. 'Come on, it's time to make our way to the reception.'

. . .

'This is a great venue.' Modeen gazed around the courtyard, taking in the profusion of leafy real plants softening the *trompe-l'oeil*-decorated walls, the statue of Venus pouring water from an urn into the central pond, the glimpse of stars through the vine-covered timbered roof of the pergola.

Emily nodded. 'The *Italian Courtyard* is very popular for weddings. Anne-Marie had to book months in advance.'

They made their way to the bar and found Peter Walters perched on a stool with two empty Crown Lager bottles in front of him.

Catching sight of Modeen, he yelled, 'There's a tab! You can get anything you want, even spirits!'

She grimaced inwardly. 'Peter, do you know Ben and Emily Logan?'

He shook his head. 'Heard Jenny speak about you is all.'

'Ben is the bride's big brother.'

Fixing the other man with a steely gaze, Ben extended a large hand, which Peter shook.

'Big alright.' Peter gazed in awe at Ben as the barman placed two full Crown Lagers and a glass of champagne on the bar. Wincing, Peter yanked his hand out of Ben's vicelike grip and threw him an accusing frown. Mumbling, 'Talk to you later,' he collected the drinks and rose to his feet. 'Gotta make sure the missus gets her bubbly.'

With an amused glance at her husband, Emily left

the baby with him while she went to check on the seating arrangements.

Ben caught the barman's eye. 'A champagne, and one … make that two … Scotch 'n Cokes, thanks.' He looked enquiringly at Modeen and received a nod of approval.

The barman had just served their drinks when Emily returned to announce, 'I've checked the seating chart.' With a sympathetic glance at Modeen she said, 'You're at that table, Jo,' and pointed to where Peter sat downing the second of his two beers. 'Ben and I are at the Logan family table.'

'Right.' Gritting her teeth, Modeen made her way reluctantly to her assigned place. Luckily for her, Peter chose that moment to return to the bar.

She was about to pull out her chair when a young man at a nearby table rose and did the honours. 'Hi, I'm Michael.' He smiled into her eyes.

'Jo.' She returned the smile and shook his extended hand.

'Nice grip,' he said with satisfaction. 'I hate limp hand shakes, they give me the heebee jeebees.'

'Yeah they give me the creeps too.'

Michael proved to be pleasant company, more so than Peter who spent most of the time at the bar while Jenny was busy with bridesmaid duties. Their entrées came and went, then the main meal followed by speeches, dessert, and finally dancing to the lively music of an accomplished four piece band.

As was usual when she attended crowded social events, Modeen found it hard to relax, and at every chance, got up to stand at the back of the room from where she had a good view. If modern warfare had taught her anything, it was that anyone could be a potential enemy.

Military training isn't something one can simply drop and leave on the battle field, she pondered. *It infiltrates every aspect of life.*

She kept a visual on Peter, watching him become more intoxicated as the night went on, and trying to chat up any woman within earshot. At one stage, Michael came looking for her to ask for a dance. When she tactfully declined, he moved on and didn't ask again. He was nice enough, but she wasn't interested in forging new friendships. She still felt the sting of losing too many close friends in action, and preferred keeping her own company most of the time.

It was safer that way.

At around midnight, a weary Jenny came looking for her. 'Hey Jo, I'm going to grab Peter. Are you ready to go?'

'Ready when you are.' Modeen tilted her chin toward the bar. 'Peter's up there.'

As they made their way through the cluster of chicken-dancing bodies on the dance floor, the two women were swept into the happy mayhem. Jenny was out of breath by the time they reached the bar.

Still laughing, she grabbed Peter by the arm. 'Come on Pete, time to go.'

He jerked his arm free, slurring, 'I'll jush … finish m'beer,' and downed the remains of the bottle, spilling some on his shirt as he did so.

Modeen looked on in disdain as he leered at her drunkenly and then sniffed and wiped the dribbles off his chin with an unsteady hand.

'C'mon, Love,' Jenny said kindly, 'let's go home.' She took him by the arm and led him, burping loudly and weaving on his feet, to the car. Reaching into his pocket, she grabbed the car keys and hit the button to unlock the doors.

'We'll let Pete have the back seat, Jo,' she murmured, 'you can sit up front with me.'

After they'd helped him into the car Jenny fastened his seatbelt, but as soon as she and Modeen were seated in the front, he undid the belt and leaned forward to thrust his head between them.

Squawking, 'Home old girl, and don't spare the horses!' he dissolved into high-pitched giggles and fell back against the seat.

Jenny rolled her eyes. 'Pete! Put your belt back on.'

'Yeah … right. Don't wan' the boys in blue pullin' us over.' He gave a raucous laugh and fumbled for the belt, while the two women exchanged pained glances.

* * *

When they arrived back at the house, Jenny said brightly, 'Right, who's for a nightcap? Tea, coffee or hot chocolate?'

'I'll have a coffee.'

'Sure, Jo.'

''N I'll 'ave a beer.'

Jenny's smile faded as she cajoled, 'Don't you think you've had enough for tonight, Pete?'

'I'll *hick* be the best judge of that.' He slumped into a chair and gave a loud burp.

'Manners, Pete! We have a guest.'

'Ish that what she ish?' He leered at Modeen who eyed him with silent contempt.

'Come on Love, why don't you have a nice cup of tea?'

'No!' He thumped the table with both fists. 'I want a freakin' BEER.'

Jenny raised her hands defensively. 'Okay, okay,' she soothed, 'no need to get upset.'

'Then stop stuffin' 'round and get me that flamin' beer!'

Scurrying to the fridge, Jenny grabbed a can and handed it to Peter. Glaring at her as he snatched the can, he pulled the ring top and made a point of taking a big swig, allowing beer to run down his chin and onto the table.

Swallowing and blinking hard, Jenny turned away and finished making hot drinks for herself and

Modeen, who had taken a seat at the head of the table where she could keep a close eye on both of them.

After a bit, Jenny sniffed and turned to say with forced brightness, 'Wasn't Anne-Marie's wedding dress just gorgeous?'

Crushing his empty can in one hand and slamming it onto the table, Peter growled, 'Well if that's all y'gonna talk about, I'm off t'bed. 'N I'll take another beer for the road … er … stairs.' He threw Modeen a sideways smirk while Jenny rushed to get him another beer. When she held out a chilled can, he grabbed it and snarled, 'And don't *you* be long.' Ripping it open, he rose unsteadily to his feet and stomped off, dripping beer froth on the floor as he went.

Without finishing her tea, Jenny put her mug in the sink. 'I'd better not keep him waiting. Goodnight, Jo. We'll talk about the wedding in the morning.'

'Sure, Jen.' Modeen was about to say more, but bit her tongue.

She stayed seated at the table until she'd finished her coffee. Rising, she rinsed out her mug, checked the back door was locked, turned off the kitchen light and quietly made her way upstairs.

As she drew near the master bedroom, she heard raised voices followed by a loud slap, a suppressed cry, and the sound of crashing furniture. Flinging open the door, she found a swaying Peter standing over Jenny, who was cowering in a corner, sobbing and nursing the side of her reddening face.

When Modeen advanced into the room, Peter turned and jabbed his index finger at her. ''N if you give me any lip, *security guard,* you can pack your bags 'n go.'

As he made to shove her out the door, Modeen grabbed his hand in a wrist lock that brought him to his knees with a howl of pain. She followed through with a knee to the chin, and his head snapped back and hit the end of the bed with a sickening thud. He blinked, sat up, and touched the side of his mouth. Seeing blood on his fingers, he swore crudely and tried to get to his feet, but Modeen stepped forward and knocked him back down with an elbow to the temple.

'Right, I've had enough of this.' Grabbing a handful of his hair, she twisted his right arm behind his back, hauled him to his feet, and proceeded to frogmarch him down the stairs. When they reached the bottom floor, she increased speed and rammed him face-first into the rear of the front door. Sinking to his knees in the corner with a strangled moan, he covered his broken nose with his free hand as Modeen opened the door.

'I don't care where you go,' she snarled into his battered face, 'but you're not staying here tonight.' With that, she shoved him out the door and down the front steps.

'Hey! You can't kick me outta my own house!'

As the door slammed closed behind him, he heard the key turn decisively in the deadlock.

CHAPTER FOUR

Jenny sat on the edge of the bed, head in hands, shoulders shaking as sobs racked her body. Hearing Modeen enter the room, she lifted her head to fix red-rimmed, tormented eyes on the guest who'd just thrown her husband out on the street.

'What have you done?' she wailed. 'What have you *done?*'

'It's over, Jen, he's gone. Everything's alright now.' Sinking onto the bed, Modeen put an arm around her shoulders. 'Are you badly hurt?'

She gave a loud sniff and ran the back of an arm across her face. 'I'll be alright.'

Grabbing a handful of tissues, Modeen handed them to her. 'You don't have to put up with abuse like that, you know.' She reached over to tie the torn ends of one of Jenny's shoulder straps back together. 'And I don't think that was the first time, was it?'

Jenny gingerly blew her nose without answering.

'This is your chance to stop it for good, to cut him loose.'

'B-but he's my h-husband.'

'Husbands don't beat up on their wives and treat them like doormats. At least not the ones that are worth keeping.' Modeen gave her a one-armed hug and stared into her face. 'You don't have to be a victim anymore.'

Jenny shook her head vehemently. 'He's only going to come back and take this out on me.' She cleared her throat and swallowed. 'And even if I left here, where would I go … what would I do?'

'You're lucky, you have friends and family to help you through this and back onto your feet. All you have to do is say the word and Peter will never bother you again.'

At that, Jenny lifted her chin and her sobs subsided into hiccups. Modeen took that as a good sign and got to her feet.

'Look, why don't you change out of that bridesmaid finery while I make us another cuppa. When you're ready, come down to the kitchen and we'll talk some more.'

A look of fear crossed Jenny's face.

'Don't worry,' Modeen assured her, 'I'll stay close by. Anyway, I doubt Peter will come back tonight,' adding under her breath, 'if he knows what's good for him.'

When a more composed Jenny joined her in the kitchen, Modeen gave an approving nod and finished making her cup of tea. Sitting across the table from her, she ran her eyes over Jenny's puffy face. She was going to have a doozy of a bruise, and probably a black eye or two. But there didn't appear to be anything broken.

The two women sat quietly talking until Jenny's eyelids started to droop.

Modeen rose. 'It's late. We should hit the hay. Wait here while I check the house is secure.'

When she returned a few minutes later, they made their way upstairs.

At the door to the master bedroom, Modeen asked gently, 'Will you be okay?'

Regarding her with serious but dry eyes, Jenny murmured, 'Yep,' adding, 'thanks Jo,' as she stepped into the room and closed the door with a soft click.

Grabbing the Nokia Ben had given her, Modeen sent off a quick text the next morning.

Suspicions confirmed last night. Problem evicted.

She got dressed and was about to head downstairs when she heard the phone ping with a return text.

Roger. Will take it from here.

In the kitchen, she put the kettle on and found a loaf of bread. She had just put two slices into the toaster when Jenny came into the room.

'Morning Jen. How're you feeling?'

'Okay … I guess.' She sat at the table and touched fingertips to her cheek. 'Though I woke up with a thumper of a headache, and my face is throbbing.'

Modeen glanced at her. 'Yeah, it looks sore. Got some painkillers?'

'I've already taken a couple.'

Nodding, Modeen turned back to the whistling kettle. 'How did you sleep?'

'Alright … surprisingly.' Jenny sobered. 'Guess I felt safe knowing you were in the room next door.'

'Good. Now, wanna cuppa?'

'Thanks.'

They were just starting on their second pieces of toast when they heard the rumble of motorcycles pulling onto the verge in front of the house.

Jenny's hand flew to her mouth and she gasped, 'Oh no, it's Pete! And his bogan mates.'

'Are you sure?'

She nodded, her eyes wide and fearful. 'I know the sounds of their Harleys.' Gripping the edge of the table with shaking hands, unwittingly ruining her mani-cured nails on the fashionably distressed timber, she made as if to rise.

Modeen was already on her feet. She checked the back door was still locked and waved a quaking Jenny back into her seat. 'Whatever happens, you stay in here. And don't open the door for anyone. You got that?'

The blood had drained from Jenny's face, leaving it

ashen under the developing bruise. She gave a distraught nod and sank back into the chair, her white-knuckled hands still clutching the table's edge. When a fist pounded on the front door, making the crockery jiggle on the table, her grip tightened and she gave a whimper, squeezing her eyes tightly closed.

Modeen strode to the door and unlocked it. Pulling it open, she took care to position herself in the doorway as she looked down into Peter's menacing eyes. Two burly men in denim and leathers stood beside him on the front porch. One of the brutes was slapping a knuckle-duster against the palm of his hand.

'Right, you've had your fun,' Peter growled, his words nasal. 'Now get the hell outta my house.'

Modeen remained where she stood, arms folded, dispassionately eyeing the visitors. When her gaze fell on Peter's shiner and the rough dressing over his swollen nose, her mouth tipped upward in one corner and she lifted a mocking eyebrow.

Seeing that, an enraged Peter snarled, 'Right!' and thumped a meaty fist into his other hand. 'Moose, Spider, get her out.' With a triumphant smirk, he moved aside to make way for the two thugs.

Modeen stepped back into the foyer so they had to come at her in single file. At six foot two, and around one hundred and forty kilos, Moose blocked out the sun as he came through the doorway. Unshaven, reeking of a mixture of stale alcohol and body odour, he reached for Modeen, a cruel set to his thin lips, only to have her intercept his hand and wrench it backward.

'Ah, AHHH!' Like a sagging, deflated balloon, he slumped to one knee in an attempt to ease the pressure on his wrist, as the second man stepped in behind him.

At just over six foot and around one-twenty kilos, Spider was no slouch either, and had a sinewy toughness about him Moose lacked.

She couldn't afford to cut this bloke any slack.

Keeping the pressure on Moose's hand, Modeen stepped around him and kicked the advancing Spider in the groin. With a grunt of pain, he grabbed his crotch with both hands and dropped to his knees beside Moose on the floor. Modeen immediately followed up with a left foot round-house kick to his temple, knocking him out cold.

Moose had taken advantage of the distraction to slip his flick knife from a pocket with his free hand. But as he raised his arm, Modeen applied more pressure to his other wrist, making him cry out. His free hand opened of its own volition and the knife dropped obligingly into Modeen's waiting palm. Flicking the blade open, she inverted the knife and drove it deep into his shoulder. With a bellow of pain, Moose threw back his head as Modeen kept up the impetus with a knee to the chin. The blow sent him backward on top of Spider with a mouthful of broken teeth.

Slapping her hands together, she eyed the mound of unconscious man flesh on the floor and then allowed her gaze to slide across to Peter. He stood in the same spot, mouth agape, eyes registering his shock and disbelief. When Modeen took a step toward him, he gave a start and backed away, almost falling down the front stairs in his haste.

'You're a bit rusty, JD.'

With a jolt, Modeen whipped around to see Ben striding down the hallway toward her.

'Should always watch your six, you know that.' Throwing her a wink, he brushed past to bend and grab the unconscious Moose by the back of his pants. Dragging him down the stairs, he heaved him onto the footpath. When he came back up, Ben squatted beside Spider and checked for a pulse.

'He'll live.' As he dumped Spider beside Moose, Ben caught sight of Peter haring down the road as though every bad-tempered Doberman in the city was snapping at his heels. Turning to look up at Modeen with a gleam of amusement in his dark eyes, he said, 'Nice going all the same.'

As he stepped over the inert bodies on his way back into the house, she enquired mildly, 'When did you get here? And how did you get inside?'

'We pulled in at the side of the house just as these apes showed up.'

'We?'

'Emily's in the kitchen with Jenny. She let us in the back door ... eventually. It took some fast talking 'cos apparently you told her not to let *anyone* in.'

'Ah.' Modeen threw him a mock-contrite glance. 'So, what about *him?*' and she indicated the fast-disappearing Peter.

'Don't worry, I'll catch up with him later.' Ben stepped into the foyer and closed the door. 'Now, before we join the ladies in the kitchen, I'd like a quick word.'

'The proposition?'

'Exactly.' He led her into the lounge room and closed the door behind them. 'These days I work for NatSec as a team leader.'

She frowned. 'NatSec?'

'A national security organisation affiliated with the Australian Intelligence Service. NatSec plans, funds and executes covert operations, and is well resourced. As team leader I get to pick my teams and I can also be choosy about the missions.'

She squinted at him sideways. 'What sort of missions are we talking about?'

'Rescues, protection and security services, intel gathering … that sort of thing. NatSec is usually called in when diplomacy and other methods fail.'

'So you're not just a glorified assassin?'

'No.' Fixing her with a level gaze, he added, 'Although some might call us that.' He gave a humourless snort. 'The Army uses the term soldiers, but what's in a name? Make no mistake, we don't whack anyone that doesn't deserve whacking.'

Modeen narrowed her eyes and gave a slow nod.

'If you're in,' Ben continued, 'there'll be three months of induction training. With your skills it'll be a breeze. You'll even get to work with some of the guys from our old unit.'

'Yeah? Like who?'

'Spooky, Wolf and Bugs. But that's about all I can tell you 'til you're in. You know, national security 'n all.'

'What about Gator? I'd like a chance to get that twenty bucks he still owes me.' Her grin faded when Ben remained solemn.

'Gator signed on for another two years,' he said slowly, 'and went MIA on his final mission.'

'Oh.' Modeen frowned. 'MIA, not KIA?'

'They never recovered his body.'

Hanging her head, she stared silently at the floor. After a long moment she raised her eyes to meet Ben's. 'So, this new gig of yours, is it worth it?'

'Well, we get to make a difference and contribute to the nation's wellbeing, which makes it worth it in my books. But you have to decide for yourself. I'll give you a couple of weeks to consider my offer.'

'Okay. So … what happens to Jenny now? What if Peter and his bogan mates decide to come back in the meantime?'

'Don't worry, we'll keep track of them, and Jenny's going to stay with us until things are settled. Emily's arranging that with her now. We'll make sure Peter agrees to a quick divorce and a fair splitting of their assets. She's gonna be fine.'

Modeen gave a brisk nod. 'Good.'

'I really appreciate your help with this, JD.' He shook his head at her. 'You're wasted as a security guard, you know. I'd really like you to be part of my team. We could use the Modeen factor.'

She gave a bark of laughter and went to hand him back the Nokia.

'Keep it, and call me if you decide you want in.'

Jenny had just gone upstairs and the other three were sitting at the kitchen table, mugs of hot drinks at their elbows, when they heard one of the motorbikes fire up outside.

Ben muttered, 'Reckon they'll be riding two-up to the hospital, to get that blade out of Boofhead's shoulder.' He took a sip of coffee and glanced at Emily. 'So it's all settled? Jenny's coming to stay with us?'

Emily nodded. 'She's putting some things together now. I told her she can stay in our downstairs guest room as long as she likes. It'll be nice to have some grown-up female company for a change.'

Ben turned to Modeen. 'You still okay to hang around here for a bit?'

'Yeah, I'll keep an eye on the place 'til first thing Wednesday morning. That'll give me a couple of days to catch up with those friends of mine.'

'Right. I'll arrange for someone to housesit after you've gone.' He waved a tattooed, muscular arm around the room. 'Don't want a nice place like this trashed out of spite.' Sitting forward, he said jauntily, 'Now, where are we going for lunch? My shout.'

At a trendy café a couple of days later, Modeen was wondering how many more baby photos she'd be expected to coo over, and how much longer she'd have to sit through the chatter about unreliable babysitters, overcrowded kindergartens, and exorbitant private school fees. Her two friends had joined the 'married with kids' set, and were very different people from the fun-loving, irresponsible girls she'd got into strife with at school.

They seemed contented enough in a stressed-out sort of way, sitting there in their milk vomit-daubed blouses. Modeen was happy for them, but found it a strain keeping the conversation from relapsing into comparisons of morning sickness woes, birthing suite horror stories, and the stomach-turning perils of potty training.

She gave a jaded sigh and drained her wine glass. *This really isn't my scene, I'd rather be back on my old security patrol.* She pursed her lips. *Though ... will I be able to handle the boredom after this weekend's excitement? I've got the old hunger for adventure back.*

Rubbing her chin, she mused, *it's great knowing I still*

have my skills, even if they have got a bit rusty. And now I've been offered an opportunity to put them to good use….

'… can't linger too long,' her friend was saying between rushed mouthfuls of Greek salad, '… I have a big clean-up job waiting for me at home.' Still chewing, she pulled a face. 'I went to get junior out of his cot this morning, only to find he'd been using the contents of his nappy to finger-paint the walls.'

Ugh! Modeen shuddered. *That's it, I've reached my limit. There's only so much a battle-hardened digger can take.*

Her breath was visible in the chill early morning air as she bent to lock the panniers. Looking forward to being back on the highway again, Modeen put the key in the ignition and pressed the start button. The motor awoke with a growl.

Giving the bike time to warm up, she took a last look around the pretty courtyard and the now unoccupied terrace house that had been her home for the last four days. Confident Jenny Walters had a brighter future to look forward to, she gave a slow smile.

And speaking of the future….

Reaching into her jacket pocket, she pulled out the Nokia and sent Ben a quick text.

I'm in.

CHAPTER FIVE

After once more checking into the Esplanade Hotel in Batemans Bay on her return journey, Modeen checked the messages on her phone. As expected, there was one from Ben.

Commence in 3 weeks. Will email details.

Flicking the phone closed, Modeen sat back and stared at it.

Well, that's it. Three weeks of 'normality' and then I start my new career as a covert operative, a NatSec 'asset'. She gave a snort. *That'll make an interesting entry on my CV.*

———

Nosing the GTR into the complex's basement garage the following evening, she removed her helmet and turned off the ignition. After dismounting stiffly, she took a deep breath and lifted her arms above her head, reaching for the concrete ceiling. It felt good to stretch, to be home again, to have helped Ben fix Jen Walters' problem, to have a new career ahead of her.

It was all good.

Sighing, she bent to unclip the panniers from the warm, ticking bike and strolled to the lift. After punching in the number for the penthouse floor, she rolled her shoulders as the lift carried her smoothly to the top of the building. Once inside her unit, she unpacked and did a workout in her private gym, before treating herself to a quick bite and a long shower.

After changing into a fresh pair of tracky pants and cropped tee, she pulled back the covers and slipped into bed, where she opened her laptop and checked her emails.

Thursday 15:17:49

From: Ben Logan <BetaTeam1@NatSec.org.au>
To: Jo Modeen <Modeen@Fastmail.com.au>
Re: Training schedule
Qantas e-tickets and itinerary attached.
Mon 1st: Swanbourne training facility Perth, WA
11th: Duntroon facility Canberra, ACT
19th: Nowra, NSW
6th – 28th: Team Facility Melbourne, VIC
Funds deposited into your account to cover

expenses. Confirm receipt and acceptance of above by return email.

NB: Require current passport photo ASAP.

BL

Modeen ran her eyes over the agenda.

Three weeks to get things in order before I'm off for a stint on the range, a week of fitness, and a parachuting refresher. Then it looks like I might have a week off, followed by almost a month-long NatSec induction.

After logging into online banking, she checked the balance of her main bank account. Sure enough, a deposit had been made by NS Trust Fund, to the sum of $10,000.00.

Three weeks later, a tee shirt and jeans-clad Modeen strode into the departure lounge at Coolangatta Airport just as her flight to Perth, via Melbourne, was being called. She joined the queue boarding the plane and slipped into her exit row seat, glad to avoid the cramped confines and knee-crushing seats in 'cattle class'.

On arrival in Perth mid-afternoon, she collected her baggage at the carousel and made her way to the exit, where she saw a young man in Army fatigues holding a white cardboard sign with MODEEN scrawled across it in bold letters. When she stopped in front of him, he leaned to the side to see around her.

She leaned with him.

He stepped to the side in annoyance.

She tapped his sign with a finger. 'Modeen,' she said flatly, 'that's me.'

He looked her up and down and snapped to attention. 'Sorry Ma'am, I was told to collect a Joe Modeen, so….'

She gave a long-suffering sigh. 'You were expecting a man.'

'Yeah.'

'I get that a lot.' She regarded him levelly. 'You got a name, soldier?'

'Private McKenzie, Ma'am.' He dipped his head to touch the brim of his slouch hat. 'Can I take your baggage?' When she handed over a khaki duffel bag, he said politely, 'Follow me, Ma'am.'

Once outside the terminal, they climbed into an Army single cab G-wagon and made their way down Great Eastern Highway. After crossing the Swan River, they motored along Mounts Bay Road toward the Campbell Barracks military base, situated next to the beach at Swanbourne.

When they pulled up outside the administration building, she remained in the vehicle, running her eyes over the base and thinking it hadn't changed much since she was last there. That was during her SASR training, when she'd first met Spooky, Wolf … and

Gator. Lowering her head, she pressed her lips together.

The training was intense – way over the top according to Gator – but those were good times.

Looking up, she saw McKenzie had grabbed her duffel and was leading the way inside.

At their approach, the desk clerk eyed her and announced, 'I take it you're the lady I've been ordered to treat like a VIP.'

'I hope so,' Modeen replied. 'Where can I stash my gear?'

Raising an eyebrow, the clerk said drily, 'This is the Army, Ma'am. There's paperwork to complete first. You'll have to sign here, here, and here.' He penned crosses on three Army admin forms. 'I'll also need to take a copy of your driver's licence. When we're finished here, Private McKenzie can give you a quick orientation of the facility.'

Formalities over, the clerk bundled up the paperwork and said briskly, 'Dinner is in the mess hall at eighteen hundred hours, lunch at twelve, and breakfast at o-six hundred. Here is your itinerary and a map of the facility. Enjoy your stay Ma'am.'

Private McKenzie led her to a row of self-contained units and unlocked unit number three. He handed Modeen the keys, saying pleasantly, 'If you'd like to stow your gear, I'll come back in about half an hour and take you on that tour. I've gotta go check the vehicle back in.' At her nod, he dipped his head and strode away.

Stepping inside, she unzipped her duffel and glanced around the single room unit. It was compact, clean, and comfortable enough with a single bed, built-in wardrobe, bathroom, and a mini kitchen. She gave a nod of satisfaction.

Luxurious compared to some barracks I've stayed in. And at least I'm not expected to bunk with the regular soldiers.

She stowed her gear and looked over the itinerary.

After we finish our tour of the base, it'll be time to head to the mess hall and grab some tucker. Tomorrow it's up at o-five hundred for a run with the Special Forces guys – that'll test my fitness, she smiled wryly *– before hitting the rifle range after breakfast. Wednesday … urban combat training at the urban complex. Thursday … counter-terrorism training and close quarter combat at the electronic CQ ranges. Friday … at the outdoor sniper range, and then departing at sixteen hundred hours to fly to Canberra.*

Yep … feels a lot like I'm back in the Army.

After waking before the four-thirty alarm, Modeen rose to take a quick shower and slip on a pair of camouflage cargo pants and her old SASR tank top. She took ten minutes to do some warm-up stretches in her room before jogging to the admin building. As she came around the corner of the building she saw six soldiers warming up on the grass. A sharp-eyed sergeant stood nearby, watching them.

As she drew closer and slowed to a walk, the sergeant looked up to stare at her and she gave a smiling nod. 'G'day Sarge.'

Sergeant John Callahan's stern expression lifted as he rocked back on his heels, hands on hips. 'Well I'll be! If it isn't Jo Modeen. Aren't you a sight for sore eyes.' He extended a hand. 'It's great to see ya.'

His unusually warm tone had the rest of the group pausing to ogle the new arrival. One of the men sniggered, 'Nice ass,' while another said, 'Pity it'll be so far behind us we won't be able to see it.'

Roaring, 'DID I TELL YOU TO SPEAK?' Callahan turned back to Modeen, who rolled her eyes. They shared a wry glance and then he said pleasantly, 'So you're joining the lads on a run this morning.'

'I am.'

'Good. You remember the fifteen kilometre track?' At her nod he winked and gave a 'get going' inclination of his closely shaved head.

Waiting just long enough to throw him an impish grin, she took off at a run.

When the six men leapt up as if to follow her, Callahan yelled, 'AS YOU WERE!' stopping them in their tracks. 'I didn't give you permission to leave. DROP and give me FIFTY!'

. . .

Modeen eased into a comfortable stride, monitoring her breathing rate in the crisp morning air as she settled in for the run. Her thoughts drifted back six years to when she'd taken the gruelling SASR entrance test. Out of a small group of twenty seasoned soldiers only sixteen had made it through the first week, and of that sixteen only five completed the gruelling course. What a thrilling result for her to be one of the five, and the first woman admitted into Australia's elite Special Forces.

The sound of ocean waves reached her ears as she followed the track leading past the back of the rifle range, and her nose caught the smell of decaying seaweed at the four kilometre marker. The trail wound through the sand dunes and onto Swanbourne beach, where it ran straight in the heavy sand for another two kilometres before winding back through the dunes to the admin building.

The first of two laps.

Just before heading through the dunes, she glanced over her shoulder and saw a group of five soldiers about a kilometre back.

Five? There should be six.

She took another look and spotted a lone soldier who'd broken away from the pack. He was about five hundred metres behind and closing fast, obviously intending to overtake her. She shook her head.

It's a mistake. If I've learnt anything during my military training, it's that success depends on teamwork.

Resisting the competitive urge to increase speed, Modeen kept the same rhythm and pace as she ran through the dunes and past the admin building. She was heading toward the four kilometre marker again when she heard the soldier close in behind her. Breathing heavily, he raced past and disappeared through the dunes.

Wow, this guy's either super fit or super competitive … and my money's on the latter. He's already puffing and still has a way to go.

Emerging from the dunes a short time later, she started the two kilometre beach stretch for the final time and saw the soldier three-quarters of the way down the track. He was on his knees, hurling his party-digested breakfast onto what had been pristine white sand.

Sailing past him, she called breezily, 'Nice going, *Chuck.'*

Pride forced him to his feet again and he made to follow, only to be overtaken by another convulsion. He dropped back to his knees, heaving, as vomit ran down his chin and dripped onto his tee shirt.

When the group of five arrived back at the admin building, they found Modeen reminiscing about old times with Sergeant Callahan. He ran his eyes over the group and yelled, 'WHERE THE HELL IS REBOLT?'

The least out-of-breath man replied, 'Down on the beach, sir. Throwing up his guts, sir.'

Callahan swallowed a grin to say sternly, 'You never, *ever* leave a team member behind. Now go back and get him.'

With groans and mutters of, 'Bloody Rebolt,' the group turned to walk back the way they'd come, only to have their sergeant yell, 'ON THE DOUBLE! And carry him back if you have to.' As the reluctant men jogged off, Callahan turned to Modeen and muttered, 'Same shit, just a different day.' He shook his head. 'I'll have to hang around here for the lads. Meet you in the mess for some brekkie, say twenty minutes?'

She nodded. 'Sounds good to me,' and made her way to her unit to shower and change. Her stomach was growling as she headed to the mess hall a short time later and lined up in the queue. Running her eyes over the food selection, she pulled a face.

Oh man, they're still serving powdered eggs. Whoever thought they were a good idea?

'Ma'am?'

She turned from her culinary inspection to find one of the soldiers from the morning's run standing behind her looking ill at ease.

'Sarge asked if you'd like to join us at our table. It's over there.' He indicated the rear of the hall.

'Okay.' Collecting her tray, she made her way to the table. When she saw who else was sitting there, she arched an amused eyebrow and took a seat. 'Hi Chuck. Feeling better?'

He squinted at her sideways and droned, 'We're training for Special Forces selection. That means pushing ourselves to the limit sometimes.' The words sounded rehearsed. Perhaps he'd been saying the same to his disgruntled mates after they'd collected him from the beach.

'But the SASR is all about teamwork,' she said evenly. 'How can you look after your team if you're too busy throwing up your guts? You need to keep that ego in check.'

Thumping the table with a fist, he growled, 'And what would a *woman* know about the SASR?'

'CUT THAT CRAP, REBOLT!' a red-faced Callahan yelled from the end of the table. 'There's only ever been one woman skilled and capable enough to join the SASR and you're looking at her. Modeen's seen active service and has been awarded the Medal for Gallantry in Action. You should be so lucky.' He pointed his fork at the chastened soldier. 'You give her some respect or I'll have you cleaning toilets with your toothbrush for the rest of the week. YOU GOT THAT?'

'Yes Sarge, sorry Sarge.' Rebolt threw Modeen a contrite glance. 'I didn't realise you're an actual member of the SASR, Ma'am.'

'*Was* a member. And apology accepted.' She gave an offhand nod as she forked a piece of toast, loaded with bacon and a daub of the detested egg, into her mouth.

'Hi, I'm Richardson.' From across the table, another of the soldiers extended a hand.

'Modeen.' She swallowed and shook his hand, as the other four introduced themselves.

'So, what action have you seen, and what's your specialisation?'

She sat back to assess Richardson and saw only sincere curiosity in his expression. 'I served in Afghanistan, Iraq, Tizak and East Timor, as signaller with Ben Logan's unit.'

'Ben Logan's unit? Wow,' a clearly awed Richardson breathed, 'you guys saw some serious action.'

Rebolt put down his cutlery to stare at her with new respect. 'So what are you doing here?'

She gave a half smile. 'Just scraping off some rust, and keeping my eye in. After this, I'm off to the rifle range for the day.'

Resting his elbows on the table, Callahan regarded her. 'Who else was in your old unit? Wait, don't tell me...,' and he sat back to stare at the ceiling. 'Logan was NCO of course, then there was ... arrhh ... Jackson, Crockman, Wolverton, and that guy with the big teeth.'

'Good memory, Sarge.' She took another mouthful of toast and followed up with a slurp of coffee.

'How're they doin'?'

'I haven't seen Spooky, Wolf, or big-teeth Bugs,' and she grinned, 'since I got out, and only just caught up with Ben about a month ago, at his sister's wedding.' Her expression grew serious again. 'And Gator … I heard he signed up for another two years but went MIA on his last tour.'

Callahan shook his head. 'That's a shame, I had a lot of respect for Crockman. An outstanding soldier, 'n brilliant with explosives.'

'Yeah.' Modeen nodded sadly. 'The best powder monkey I've worked with, and a funny guy to boot.'

Rebolt piped up, 'Crockman? His first name's Eric, isn't it?

Modeen turned to eye him. 'Did you know Gator?'

'Met him a coupl'a times. Could'a sworn I saw him in Sydney about two months ago, at a pub in Darling Harbour.' He rubbed his chin. 'Well … it looked like him, but I guess it can't have been if he's MIA.'

Modeen regarded Rebolt thoughtfully as Callahan slapped his hands and announced, 'Right, we must be off.' He got to his feet, followed by his men. Turning to smile at Modeen, he said, 'See you at dinner tonight?'

Raising her cup at him in a mock salute, she watched them file out and then rose to get a refill of coffee. When she returned to her seat, her thoughts were still on Gator.

Could Rebolt have been right about seeing him? Ben did say his body hadn't been found….

She held her cup in both hands and took a distracted sip.

Rebolt must've been mistaken. Then again….

Taking the Nokia from her back pocket, she opened the contact list and dialled Ben's number.

'JD.'

'G'day Ben. Got a question for you.'

'Fire away.'

'Do you know what actually happened to Gator, on that last mission?'

After a moment's silence Ben said slowly, 'When he signed up again, he was transferred into an advanced recon group with the Regulars.' A sombre note crept into his voice. 'They were on deployment in Iraq when he bought it. He and two others in his team entered a booby-trapped building and there was a massive explosion. Their bodies weren't recovered.'

'I see.'

'Why do you ask?'

'One of the guys here reckons he might've seen Gator in Sydney about two months ago.'

'Unlikely.' Ben paused. 'But I'll look into it, see if there's been any new developments.'

'Thanks.'

'So, how're things going?'

'Okay. But … tell me something?'

'Sure.'

'Were we ever *that* green?'

Ben gave a bark of laughter. 'You bet! I remember a

young recruit always trying to prove she was better than any of the men.' Modeen grinned wryly as he went on. 'You're on the range today?'

'Yep, starting with the Glock 17s on the pistol range. Should've brought Walt with me.'

Ben gave an amused grunt. 'Don't sweat the small stuff. You can use whatever you want when you've finished your induction. Right, seeya in a couple of weeks.'

After transferring from Campbell Barracks to Bindoon Army Base in an MRH90 chopper, Modeen made use of the base's remote weapons range to fire, among other things, a Carl Gustov recoilless rifle and an M72 LAW rocket launcher. That afternoon she was ferried back to barracks by the same chopper.

Saying her goodbyes to Sergeant Callahan at the end of the week, she joked about having fired every type of weapon the Army had to offer, just about. They laughed together and then she packed up her gear, ready to move on to Canberra for the next leg of her induction.

CHAPTER SIX

At Canberra Airport, Modeen collected her bag from the carousel while searching the crowd of passengers, and the people collecting them, for a placard with her name on it. There was none. Nor was there an expectant-looking 'uniform' hovering in the arrivals area.

Spying a café and catching the scent of freshly roasted beans on the air, she licked her lips. The coffee served on base was mostly instant, and what was offered on the plane was, in a word, *ordinary*. Tempted by the thought of a barista-made flat white, she headed for the café. May as well be comfortable while waiting for her tardy ride.

The man leaning against a pillar to her left swivelled to flick her a narrow-eyed glance as she passed. Feeling her skin prickle, she stopped and once more gazed around the arrivals hall. There were people everywhere, some strolling, some rushing, others standing looking expectant or frazzled.

None overly interested in her.

All the same, her finely-honed instincts told her to proceed with caution. She turned slowly, about to continue into the café, only to freeze at a sharp tap on her shoulder.

Spinning around, she put a hand to her chest and growled, 'Damn it, Spooky! I hate it when you sneak up on me like that.'

He gave a gleeful bark of laughter. 'But I love it, 'specially as I don't manage to do it often. Your damn "radar" gets me most times.'

After dropping her bags to give him the traditional fist-bump, she stepped back to appraise him. 'Wow, look at you dressed in a suit and all. And have you grown a few inches?'

'Hah!' He lifted a trouser leg to reveal a cowboy boot with an impressive heel. 'Check out these babies!'

She laughed. 'How've you been, Spook?'

'Good.'

'I see you haven't lost your touch.' She arched an eyebrow at him.

He shrugged. 'Stealth is my thing, you know that. You guys didn't christen me Spooky for nothin'.' They shared a grin as he went on. 'And you look as fit as ever.'

'Ta. So, what are you doing here?'

'Ben sent me to collect you.'

'Great! Well, I was about to grab a coffee, you up for one?'

'I think we can do better than coffee. Have you eaten?'

'Just some peanuts on the plane.'

Snatching up her duffel, he slung it over a compact, muscular shoulder. 'Right, let's get outta here.' Leading her across the car park toward a yellow late model Camaro, he hit the remote. The car's lights flashed and the doors unlocked. Opening the passenger side door, he announced, 'Bumblebee, at your service.'

'Nice car.' Modeen eyed him sceptically. 'A bit conspicuous though, for the line of work you're in?'

'This is my private ride.' He watched her slide into the passenger seat and then stowed her duffel in the trunk before jumping in the driver's side. 'Seafood, Italian, or something else?' He turned the key in the ignition and the ZL1 muscle car's six-point-two litre engine roared into life, settling into a deep, rumbling idle.

'I could go a steak.'

'Well, I know a great little pub not far from here that does good steaks. And afterwards we can grab a coffee at Casa De Spooky.'

'You're on.'

After they'd chatted, reminisced and laughed over dinner and a few drinks, Spooky drove them back to his high-rise apartment on Bunda Street.

Stepping onto the balcony, Modeen murmured, 'Great view.'

'Yeah.' Spooky loosened his tie and shrugged out of his jacket, slinging it over the back of a chair. 'That's Lake Burley Griffin you can see in the distance.' He went into the kitchen and Modeen heard him setting up the espresso machine she'd noticed on the bench.

She came back inside, saying, 'I can't stay too late, I've got to find a place to bunk tonight. Not sure if Ben had anything organised. The itinerary he gave me wasn't that detailed.'

'It's not like Ben to be disorganised.' Spooky snorted affably. 'He probably knew I'd invite you to stay here. I've got a spare bedroom with its own ensuite you're welcome to, for as long as you like.'

'Are you sure it's no trouble?'

'None at all. I'm supposed to deliver you to the base tomorrow by o-nine hundred anyway. Actually,' and he threw her a grin, 'having you here would mean I could sleep a bit longer in the morning.'

'It's a deal then, thanks.'

When the espresso machine began to gurgle and thump, and aromatic, caramel-coloured brew issued from the spout, Modeen left Spooky to check out her digs. After dropping her bag in a corner of the guest room, she freshened up and returned to the kitchen, to see him topping up their cups with frothed milk and making fern-leaf patterns in the dense white foam.

As he carried the coffees to the table, Modeen eyed them and smiled. 'Wow, you're quite the barista. I'm impressed.'

'I've had to multi-skill now I'm back in the world.'

'Haven't we all.'

They shared a knowing grin as he passed her a cup. 'Bottoms up.'

She stayed the whole week at Spooky's place, taking up his offer of guest room and the use of his Camaro to get around. She spent most of her time at the base, having her fitness assessed as she worked out in the gym, did laps of the pool, ran the cross country circuit, and other physical activities. After disappearing for a few days, Spooky returned in time to show her some of the city sights.

Over dinner on one of her last nights there, he announced, 'Ben reckons I could use a refresher, so I'm coming to Nowra with you.'

'Great.' She smiled broadly. 'We taking Bumblebee?'

"Fraid not. This is work, so we have to take the Aurion.'

'Oh, of course.' She slapped her forehead in a dramatic gesture.

'We'll head off on Saturday morning. Ben's booked us rooms in a motel near the parachute training academy.'

'Sounds good to me.' Sitting back, she sighed, 'I'm

ready to move on. All this physical stuff is good for fitness but can be boring if that's all you're doing.'

———

'Nowra's only about a two and a half hour drive.' Spooky loaded their gear onto the back seat of the Aurion. 'Hey, check this out,' and he beckoned her to the rear of the car. After a quick scan of the underground carpark to ensure they were alone, he opened the boot. 'This is standard issue for agent vehicles.'

He lifted the floor panel. In the spare tyre space separately lined cases held a Glock 17, an MP5SD6, and a Nemesis Arms Vanquish fifty cal sniper rifle, its detached barrel and scope lying alongside the stock.

Murmuring, 'Nice,' Modeen eyed him. 'We won't be needing them on this trip, will we?'

He shook his head. 'We're on work time, but not on assignment. We're normally given advance notice of them and time to prepare … depending on the nature of the assignment of course.' With a sideways glance at her, he pressed open the left compartment to reveal two sets of false number plates and a tool kit.

At her 'so-what?' shrug, he pressed open the right compartment and she saw a sixty-six millimetre M72 LAW anti-tank weapon cushioned snugly in a foam cut-away.

'Now you're talking.'

'Thought you'd like that.' Spooky snapped the boot shut. 'Right, let's get this show on the road.'

Setting out east to Braidwood, they took a northerly course toward Nowra. On arrival there, they pulled into a Golden Chain motel on the main highway, within sight of the academy turn-off.

For their first drop of the morning, they joined a group of ten cadets boarding a twin turbo-prop CASA C-212. The military aircraft, with its high-mounted wing, boxy fuselage, and suitability for short take-offs and landings, was ideal for paratrooper deployment.

At an altitude of one thousand feet, the harsh-voiced trainer inside the cabin directed the cadets to conduct their final checks, and then line up in single file facing the rear of the aircraft. Once satisfied his charges were connected to the static line, the trainer lowered the rear ramp and ordered them to deploy.

After the last cadet had jumped, the ramp was raised and the plane circled and continued climbing. At twelve thousand feet the pilot once more lowered the ramp. On the green signal, Modeen and Spooky jumped. After free-falling side by side, they separated and deployed their wing-shaped chutes. Turning and weaving in the air gave them a feel for the wind strength and direction.

Swooping in low over the ground, Modeen pulled down hard on the steering toggles. As her chute began to stall, she touched down lightly on target. Stepping sideways, she spun around and gathered up her chute as Spooky landed in the same spot.

He reeled in his canopy and glanced over at her. 'Nice bit of rapid descent, Modeen! Just like riding a bike isn't it?'

She grinned. 'I can think of worse ways to spend a morning.'

'Good, 'cos after lunch at the academy, we're doing the same jump from a Chinook transport chopper.'

'Never jumped out of a Chinook before.'

'Me neither.' As they made their way to the waiting support vehicle, he added, 'Which is probably why we've been instructed to do it.'

As the same group of cadets and their instructor climbed into the Chinook that afternoon, followed by Modeen and Spooky, the pilot fired up the Boeing twin turbo-shaft engines. The huge rotors lifted the chopper with ease, and at ten thousand feet the instructor readied the cadets. Catching Spooky's eye, he asked if he'd assist by dropping the rear ramp and supervising the exits. With a brisk nod, Spooky rose and made his way to the rear of the chopper, where he hooked his harness to an anchor line. On the instructor's signal, he lowered the ramp.

A buzz sounded and the green glow of the ready light filled the cabin as the first cadet stepped forward.

Tapping the young man on the shoulder, Spooky shouted, 'Go!'

The cadet jogged to the end of the ramp and dropped out of sight, the static line pulling his drogue free. Modeen moved closer to watch the white plume of his main chute balloon in the air below.

Ushering forward the second cadet, Spooky tapped his shoulder. 'Go!'

The third and fourth cadets followed in quick succession. About to usher forward the fifth, Spooky put a halting hand on the cadet's chest after glancing at Modeen, who was staring anxiously out into the sky.

Two seconds had passed without a sign of the fourth cadet's chute having opened.

Racing forward, she leapt off the ramp.

The rushing wind stung her cheeks as she took a swift scan of the expanse of blue sky. Below her three white chutes were falling leisurely … and then she glimpsed it. A fourth dark shape, plummeting toward the ground. Tucking her arms hard against her sides and pressing her legs together, she speared head-first toward the free-falling cadet.

Go belly down, kid, she thought desperately, *give me time to reach you.*

Tumbling and spinning in the fast-moving air, the cadet gave his drogue another frantic tug. This did nothing but twist him face-up … so that he was staring right at her. She saw him jerk as though hit with two-forty volts.

C'mon, kid, think!

As if he'd read her mind, the cadet twisted himself horizontal again and spread-eagled, marginally slowing his descent. Knowing she had about seven seconds before they both reached terminal velocity, she continued spearing downward, only flattening out as she closed in on him.

Their bodies collided with a dull whack.

Yelling, 'Gotcha!' in his ear as she wrapped her arms and legs around him, she snapped a locking karabiner onto his rig harness and deployed her own chute.

When the wing bit into the air, the opening shock made them grunt as the sudden yank on their harnesses punched the air from their lungs.

With two of them relying on one chute, the ground was coming up fast … too fast. Modeen worked the chute, using the wing's manoeuvrability to slow their descent until they were skimming the ground close to the target. When the chute finally stalled, they had slowed sufficiently to make a safe, if heavy, landing to cheers from observers on the ground.

They'd both managed to keep their feet on landing, but when Modeen unbuckled the karabiner the cadet gave a groan and sank to his knees, head bowed, body quivering. When she put a reassuring hand on his shoulder he looked up at her, his face pale and his eyes wide and dark.

Shaking his head in wonder, he swallowed and rasped, 'Thank you.'

'You're welcome, cadet.'

They were interrupted by the noisy arrival of the other three cadets, who'd landed safely moments after their free-falling comrade. They took turns slapping him on the back and ribbing at the top of their voices, 'Nice going, mate,' and, 'Oh *man!* 'Bout time you changed those undies!'

After the Chinook touched down again, the rest of the cadet group hurried over, throwing air punches and whooping as they made for their ashen-faced buddy. The instructor had to yell his thanks to Modeen over the commotion. Leaning in close, he added, 'There'll be an enquiry and investigation before we can go up again.'

She nodded as Spooky jogged over to join them. 'Is he alright?'

'He's fine.'

Spotting the white-faced cadet on the ground cradling his faulty rig, Spooky walked up to clap him on the back. 'Look, mate,' he said, winking to the others in the group, 'if you wanted to meet Modeen, you could've just asked.'

Everyone laughed and the tension was broken.

'Let's see that rig.' After taking the back container and harness from the cadet, Spooky examined it closely. Feeling around it with exploratory hands, he mumbled, 'This feels like it's all stuck together.' Pausing, he glanced narrow-eyed at the cadet. 'Someone got it in for you, kid?'

The young man swallowed and shrugged.

Spooky turned to Modeen. 'What happened?'

'The pilot chute wouldn't deploy for some reason. I could see him trying everything to get it open so I knew there was no point in fiddling with it, and no time to muck around either.'

'You got that right. Gutsy move, Modeen.'

'Anyone would've done the same. I was just the first to realise he was in trouble.' As they turned to make their way back to the academy she added, 'Best of all, no one got hurt and the academy's reputation remains intact.'

Spooky nodded. 'Well … after that bit of excitement, it's the classroom for us all day tomorrow. At least we're booked to do a HALO jump mid-morning Wednesday. You up for it?'

'A high altitude low open … yeah I'm up for it, although I'm not fond of freezing my butt off.' Looking back at the cadet who was now on his feet surrounded by his admiring buddies, her lips split in an impish grin. 'What could possibly go wrong?' She paused. 'How high are we jumping from?'

'Twenty-five thousand feet.' Seeing her roll her eyes, Spooky chortled, 'Just like old times, hey?'

She gave an amused snort. 'Great having you along, Spook.'

'Great being along, Modeen.'

CHAPTER SEVEN

'We're doing the jump from a C-130J Super Hercules, along with four Special Forces guys.' Spooky led Modeen into the locker room. 'They said we could use these,' and he held up two pairs of knitted long-johns. 'Figured you'd be happy about that.'

'Outstanding, Spook.' She took the pair he handed her and stripped down to her singlet and boy-leg panties. After pulling on the long-johns she slipped into a jump suit, as Spooky did the same.

On their way to the pre-jump tack room, he quipped, 'Man, I'd forgotten how much shit we have to put on for one of these jumps.'

'Just be thankful we don't have to carry the Carbines and eighty pound packs like those poor bastards,' and she pointed to the four soldiers seated across the room. After a cursory glance at them, the uniformed men resumed staring ahead with closed expressions.

'Hey, speaking of gear,' and Spooky flicked her arm with a finger, 'did you hear what came out of the investigation into the cadet's incident yesterday?'

'No, did you?'

'Yep. Turns out the rig *was* all stuck together, like I thought.'

She frowned. 'But … how? Why?'

'Apparently a painter and his apprentice were doing some varnishing in the room where a few re-packed rigs were waiting to go back into storage.' Anticipating what was coming, Modeen winced as Spooky continued. 'The young apprentice spilled a tin of varnish, and didn't tell his boss. He was on his second warning – for clumsiness I'd reckon – so he was too scared to own up. He just mopped up the stuff, not realising some of it had seeped into one of the rigs. Of course it gummed up the works and had hardened nicely by the time your young mate strapped it on.'

With an incredulous shake of her head, Modeen murmured, 'Such a simple thing … that could've ended in tragedy.'

When the time came to board the Hercules, Spooky and Modeen followed the troopers inside. All six plugged in and activated their oxygen lines for thirty minutes' intake of one hundred percent oxygen, a prerequisite for every high altitude jump. They sat inhaling the pure air as the four Rolls Royce turbo-prop engines thundered the bulky transport plane down the runway, and lifted it majestically into the air.

As they approached the jump altitude of twenty-five thousand feet, the digital READY light flashed to the beat of an audible buzzer. The six jumpers checked their AADs, bail-out oxygen, and rigs one last time, and readied themselves for the drop. Shortly afterward, a louder secondary buzzer sounded, and a red revolving beacon illuminated as the rear ramp opened. When the ramp locked into place, the buzzer stopped, leaving the jumpers tensely poised with only the drone of the plane's motors in their ears.

The lead trooper rose to his feet, followed by the other three. Modeen and Spooky slipped into place behind them. The digital READY display went solid and the audio buzzer sounded a single, drawn-out note. The display flashed twice, and changed to DEPLOY. As soon as it turned green, the first two troopers jogged forward and disappeared off the end of the ramp. They were followed three seconds later by the next two, and three seconds after that by Modeen and Spooky.

The instant they left the comparative warmth of the plane's cabin, the cold atmosphere blasted against them like a solid wall, sucking the warm air out of their lungs and leaving them gasping. Modeen blinked and shook her head to clear it as frost momentarily crusted the exterior of her visor. At that moment, she could imagine Spooky's disdain for 'all the shit they had to put on for the jump' changing to gratitude for the long-johns, helmet, gloves, and free-fall boots, all protecting them from the freezing air.

Sweeping back their arms, the six jumpers rocketed toward the drop zone at terminal velocity. At ten thousand feet, all but one of them split formation, flattened out, and deployed their chutes. Looking down, Modeen watched horrified as one of the troopers continued hurtling toward the earth, limbs flapping lifelessly around his tumbling torso.

At seven hundred and fifty feet, the trooper's automatic activation device deployed his reserve chute. It ballooned in the air, slowing his descent before depositing him on the ground in a crumpled, nerveless heap. The other three landed nearby and hurried to his side. With swift efficiency, they checked his pulse, removed the bulk of his gear, and placed him in the recovery position. Soon after, the support vehicle arrived, and the medics wasted no time putting the insentient trooper on a stretcher and loading him into the back of the wagon.

After landing a short distance away, Modeen walked over to the closest medic. 'Is he going to be alright?'

The man turned and nodded. 'Lucky for him the AAD deployed and stopped him pile-driving into the ground.'

'What happened to him?'

'We think he just blacked out during the drop. It happens every now and then, which is why we're always on standby for these HALO jumps.' After inclining his head at her, the medic hurried to catch the departing wagon.

She was watching the vehicle lurch its way across the field when a deep voice behind her said, 'Hi. We haven't been introduced.'

She turned to see one of the troopers extending a hand. 'I'm Steve Rourke.'

'Jo Modeen. And this is Luke Jackson.' She indicated Spooky with a lift of her chin and Steve threw him a nod, before turning back to her.

'We've finished our SASR induction and are awaiting our first deployment. What's your story?'

'Nothing much really,' Spooky interjected. 'We're just a couple of civilian skydivers taking it to the next level.'

Steve glanced at him sideways and narrowed his eyes. 'So how'd you manage a jump on a military flight like this?'

'We've got connections.' Wiggling his brows, Spooky tapped his index finger against the side of his nose.

That seemed to satisfy Steve. 'Y'know,' he said with a wry grin, 'it's ironic. Tony, the guy they just carted off, had dibs on the lovely lady here,' and he inclined his head toward Modeen, 'being the one to pass out on the drop.'

Seeing her arch an eyebrow, Spooky swallowed a smile to mutter, 'Yeah, she gets that a lot.' When he noticed Steve staring at Modeen, he announced cheerfully, 'Anyway, we need to head back to base. So we'll catch you later, Steve.'

After gathering up their chutes, they started walking back across the field. Half way over, Spooky leaned toward Modeen to say quietly, 'By the way, now we're with the agency, we don't use our real names.'

'Oh. Sorry, Spook, I didn't know.'

'No worries. Just givin' you a heads-up.'

'So, what do I call you?'

'I'm Luke Williams.'

'Nice to meet you, Mr Williams.' She extended a hand which he shook, and they laughed together.

'Once you've completed your induction, Ben will organise your new ID and papers. They give us fairly common surnames and usually leave our Christian names the same, to keep things simple. For security reasons, *everything* we use in agency work – our IDs, passports, bank accounts, you name it – are all in our operative names.'

'Makes sense. So, do you like the work, Mr Williams?'

He grinned. 'When there's no one around, you can still call me Spooky. And yes, I enjoy the work. It's like being in our old unit. We're a close-knit team and Ben, as you know, is a trustworthy leader. We get all the support we want, and I've never had issues with any of the assignments I've been handed.'

'Good to know.'

'Right, we'd better return this gear to the academy. After that, you okay to head back to Canberra?'

'Yep, I've had enough excitement for one week.'

They motored north the following day to Moss Vale on Nowra Road, and then South-West toward Canberra via the Illawarra Highway. After refuelling in Goulburn they set off on the last leg of their journey.

As Spooky turned left to hook up with the Federal Highway, Modeen said idly, 'You caught up with any other members of the old unit?'

'Haven't seen Bugs in a while, he's been stationed in the Middle East for the past year. Dude actually likes it over there.' Spooky threw her a half smile and shook his head. 'Takes all kinds.' Turning his attention back to the road, he said, 'Remember how picky Ben was about his squad? He must've trialled about four other highly skilled soldiers before he chose Bugs to join the unit. And it wasn't because Bugs was a tougher soldier or a better marksman than the others – though don't get me wrong, the boy's got skills – it was because he jelled with the rest of us. A logical move. Why throw a spanner into a well-oiled machine.'

She gazed at him thoughtfully. 'Seems Ben's gone

out of his way to recruit most of the members of the old unit into NatSec.'

'Which is clever when you think about it. We worked closely together as a squad, saved each others' hides more than once, and shared a solid bond of trust. Even under heavy fire we were an effective unit … none of us had to be told what to do. If we saw a hole in our defences or a weak spot in our attack, we'd just fill it. So it makes total sense that Ben would want us on his team, especially considering our skills.'

She nodded slowly. 'Guess I assumed as agents we'd mostly work alone.'

'And we often do, unless the job requires more than one operative. Even then we usually have a say about who we work with.' Spooky's face lit up. 'Hey, you might even run into Wolf down in Melbourne next week.'

She beamed. 'Cool!'

'You'll find keeping in touch with the team easy after you get your "bat phone" and other gadgets.' When she pulled out the Nokia mobile Ben had given her and held it out for him to see, Spooky laughed aloud. 'That's not a phone, it's hardly more than a personal tracker. Now *this* is a phone,' and he took out a sleek-looking, five by two-and-a-half inch unit in a black leather case. 'Standard issue, and not called a smart phone for nothing. I could show you all the neat stuff it can do, but you'll find that out during your induction. Needless to say, it's a GPS tracker, has infrared and heat imaging displays, Taser capability, and even has a decent explosive charge that you can set with the timer. Oh! And check this out.'

He reached across to tap a small button above the glove box in front of Modeen. A twelve inch monitor emerged from the dashboard, its screen displaying the white outline of a hand. Pulling onto the side of the road, Spooky placed his left hand over the outline. Modeen watched the digital hand turn green then flash as yellow shock waves radiated from each fingertip. When he removed his hand, a globe of the earth appeared on the screen with the word 'NatSec' circling it.

He said, 'Dial Peterson,' in a commanding voice, and an old-fashioned phone icon appeared on the screen. Its circular dial rotated and then the sound of a ringing phone chimed from the car's speakers. Following a loud click, the phone icon minimised onto the menu bar beside a video camera icon, as Bugs' gravelly voice issued from the speakers.

'G'day Mr Williams. What can I do for ya?'

'Got someone here you might know, Mr Peterson.' When Spooky tapped the video camera icon, Bugs' bleary-eyed, freckled face appeared on the screen. He blinked first at Spooky and then at Modeen, and let out a whoop.

'Modeen! Great to see ya. I heard rumours you might've be comin' on board.'

'Great to see you too, Bugs. Spook tells me you're in the Middle East?'

'That's right.' His lips stretched into a trademark toothy grin. 'I take it he's givin' you a run-down on the team, and introducin' you to the techo stuff?'

'He is. And I have to say, this is an impressive real-time hook-up! There's hardly any delay.'

'Yep, we get to play with some cool stuff.'

Seeing him stifle a yawn, Spooky said with a grin, 'We keeping you up, buddy?'

'As a matter of fact, yes.' Throwing him a disgruntled glance, Bugs addressed Modeen again. 'Isn't that I'm not glad to hear from you, it's just the small matter of the time difference … a detail Spook tends to forget.'

'What is the time over there?'

Bugs yawned again. 'One in the mornin'.'

'Ooh, sorry mate.' Spooky gave a guilty wince. 'My bad. We'll hang up and let you get back to sleep.'

With a mildly sarcastic, 'Kind of you,' Bugs turned to flash Modeen another grin. 'Good seein' you, Modeen. Look forward to catchin' up again later … and at a later time.' He raised an eyebrow at Spooky, who saluted and then terminated the call. When he pressed the button on top of the screen, it folded and disappeared back into the dash.

Nosing the car onto the bitumen again, Spooky accelerated to highway speed and muttered, 'That Bugs, he could sleep anywhere, anytime, and never did like being disturbed.'

'I don't think anyone appreciates being woken at that hour of the night.'

'Yeah, you're right.' He gave an amused grunt. 'I'm lucky it was Bugs and not Gator.' He shook his head. 'Remember what a grumpy buggar Crockman could be when roused? He'd wake up swinging.' When Modeen made no comment, Spooky glanced at her. 'Did you hear from him after we left the service?'

'No.' She stared down at her hands. 'I'm sure Ben would've liked to have him on the team too, but he went MIA on his last mission.'

'Yeah, I heard.' Spooky's gaze softened. 'You do know he was just teasing you about the time you grazed him with that bullet?'

'Of course.' Lifting her chin, she fixed him with narrowed eyes. 'All the same, you don't ever want to welch on a debt with me.'

They shared a smile and then Spooky asked, 'What time's your flight tomorrow?'

'O-eight hundred.'

The following morning, Spooky insisted on parking the Camaro and escorting her through airport security to the departure lounge, where he waited with her until her flight was called.

On hearing the announcement over the PA, he sighed and rose to his feet. 'Well, I guess this is it. When you see the other guys, say g'day for me. And don't forget to drop in on your way back if you get a chance.' He reached out to give Modeen the usual fist bump, only to be pulled in for a hug.

Drawing back, she smiled warmly at him. 'Thanks for your hospitality, Spook.'

'Anytime, Modeen.'

With a smiling nod, she turned and strode to the departure gate.

CHAPTER EIGHT

On arrival at Tullamarine airport, feeling refreshed after a ten minute micro-sleep during the flight, Modeen headed through the arrivals hall to baggage collection. As she neared the baggage carousel, she saw a tall figure step forward and fix her with a level gaze.

'Here, let me.' Ben took her duffel, lifting the heavy bag like it weighed nothing. 'Good flight?'

Modeen slipped into step beside him as he strode toward the exit. 'It was okay. And Spook said to say hi.'

'How's he going?'

'Fine, keeping fit.' She smiled. 'He's adjusted well to civilian life and has become quite domesticated. Even makes his own espresso coffee … and cooks! His tuna mornay is up there with the best I've had.'

Ben dipped his head. 'Good.' Once outside he looked around before saying in a low voice, 'Now, down to business. I've had a look at the reports from Swanbourne, Duntroon, and Nowra. You obviously haven't let your fitness drop since leaving the service, and your scores on the rifle ranges are still first-rate.' He paused as a harried traveller rushed past them towing an over-stuffed wheeled suitcase.

After a quick glance over his shoulder to see the traveller disappear through the terminal doors, Ben carried on. 'I've also received first-hand feedback on your performance.' His lips twitched. 'Sergeant Callahan's account of your first training run was good for a laugh. But seriously, he reckons you never fail to impress. And a One Star at Nowra went out of his way to call and compliment us on your bravery in saving that cadet. Well done, JD.'

'All in a day's work.' Modeen's cheeks flushed pink at the praise from her old unit leader, whose approval she valued more than that of a 'One Star' Air Commodore. 'Hey, how's Jenny going? Did she have any more trouble with that slob of a husband?'

'No, he's out of the picture,' Ben said flatly. 'Jenny's still staying with us, Emily and Chelsea love having her around. When the settlement on the terrace house comes through, she intends to buy a small place in the suburbs, near where Anne-Marie and Dan live. She's gone back to work and seems to be enjoying the return of her independence.'

'I'm glad things are working out for her. Here's

hoping she sticks with it and doesn't let that waste-of-space back into her life.'

Ben nodded as they made their way through the multi-storey carpark, past the usual assembly of SUVs and brightly coloured city hatches, to a dark blue Aurion. It sat low and intimidating among the other inconsequential vehicles as though poised for action.

Reaching into a pocket, Ben took out the car keys and a fat envelope, which he handed her. 'By the way, here are your papers. You're now officially Josephine Bennet. Use that alias whenever you're on assignment.'

Modeen stood turning the envelope over in her hands before climbing into the car.

As Ben negotiated the freeway traffic surging its way toward the inner city, Modeen thumbed through the contents of the envelope. On top was a passport. Opening it, she saw the photo she'd sent at his request. She gazed at it a moment, chewing her bottom lip, and then tipped the rest of the envelope's contents onto her lap. Amid the assortment of swipe cards and fobs, she found a Victorian driver's licence and a folder containing assorted bank and credit cards.

Ben glanced over. 'Hand me the plain white card.' As they turned into a narrow one-way lane nestled between two lofty buildings, he used the card to swipe them in. The boom gate lifted and they continued down a ramp. When they came to an imposing steel roller door, he pointed to the concrete wall near the driver's side. 'See that camera?'

She nodded.

'Car, driver and any other occupants will be scanned before being let in. If you're ever kept waiting here, expect to be visited by an armed guard.'

A few seconds later, they heard a loud metallic clunk and the door groaned open. With a fleeting squeal of fat tyres on concrete, Ben guided the Aurion into the subterranean carpark.

Peppered with solid concrete pillars supporting the towering structure above, and surprisingly well-lit and ventilated, the carpark was large enough to cater for thirty vehicles. Modeen's lips tipped upward at the corners when Ben pulled into the parking space marked SMITH. Five identical Aurions sat alongside with three black, menacing-looking 4WD troop carriers down the line from them.

As they exited the vehicle Ben grabbed her duffel and led the way to the lift. He held up her swipe card and then ran it over a blank panel to the right of the lift door. An upward arrow pulsed green and stopped as the door opened. Handing back the card, he said, 'Same one for the boom and the lift.'

'Roger that.' As they stepped into the elevator, she eyed the control panel. 'This thing only goes down one level?'

'Correct.' He waited while she pressed the button.

Three seconds later the door opened and they

stepped out. 'Wow, that was quick.' She threw him a grin. 'And no canned music.'

They walked down the corridor, their footsteps echoing off the highly-polished surfaces. At the far end of the corridor a security guard manned a counter behind a thick glass screen. A revolving door sat immobile to the left of the counter. Beside it, a small conveyor belt led to a scanner unit on the other side of the glass.

The poker-faced guard looked up at their approach. 'Please identify yourselves.'

Ben stepped up to a podium with a digital display containing the outline of a hand, like the one Modeen had seen in Spooky's car. Placing his left hand on the screen he said clearly, 'Ben Smith.' The outline turned green and flashed as threadlike yellow shock waves radiated from each fingertip.

'Identity confirmed,' a robotic voice announced from a speaker on the side of the podium.

Ben turned to address the guard. 'I have a new recruit for processing,' and he placed Modeen's duffel on the conveyor. The belt hummed into life, and the bag rolled away to disappear through the curtain of rubber straps at the mouth of the scanner.

'One moment, sir.' The guard picked up a phone and muttered a few words.

As he hung up, a large panel on the left of the corridor opened abruptly, and a man dressed in a black suit and carrying an MP5 emerged. He eyed them before pointing the rifle at the ceiling and stepping aside, indicating for them to go through the door.

Ben glanced at Modeen. 'We need to get you scanned and squared away.'

She followed him into an anteroom roughly five metres wide by eight metres long. Behind them the black-suited guard pulled the door closed as another similarly dressed man, also armed with an MP5, approached them holding a hand-held scanner.

In response to the man's polite, 'May I?' Ben unbuttoned his jacket and held it open, revealing a Glock 17 nestled in a leather shoulder holster.

The guard threw him a bemused look and shook his head. 'No point in scanning you, Mr Smith.' He turned to Modeen, who extended her arms while he ran the scanner over her. Stepping back, he gave a satisfied nod. 'Clear.'

At a large desk on the near side of the room, a technician in his mid-forties sat amid a bunch of electronic equipment, tapping on a keyboard and scooting a wireless mouse around a NatSec mouse pad. Hearing them approach, he pushed his thickly-rimmed glasses back up his nose and without looking at the visitors, indicated the table and chairs in the centre of the room. 'Please take a seat.'

When he finally raised his eyes, he did a double take and gave a low whistle. 'Whoa! You neglected to tell me we were getting such a good-looking addition,

Ben.' He rose to his feet and extended a hand to Modeen. 'Hi, I'm James. James O'Neill.'

Modeen gave his hand a firm shake. 'Josephine Bennet.'

'Nice to meet you, Josephine. Can I see your passport and keycards please?'

As she handed them over, James turned to Ben. 'We'll be about an hour. I'll bring her down to your office when we're done.'

With a dip of his head, Ben strode to the wall at the back of the room. Seeing the outline of a panel in the wall, but no handle or knob, Modeen watched as Ben swiped his access card. The panel opened inward with a loud clunk, and after he disappeared through it, closed behind him with another solid thud.

Noticing her interest, James said, 'You'll normally use the revolving door to enter the building, like the rest of us plebs.' He slapped his hands together. 'Right, let's finish entering your details into the system. Your access card's only programmed to get you this far at present. For the rest of the building we'll need to step up your access levels.' His fingers flew over the keyboard, and then he sat back and waved a hand in the air like a magician brandishing a wand. 'Done and done.'

He opened the door of a small booth at the end of the table. 'Now we need a full body scan. Can you step inside please?' After she entered the booth, he said, 'I need you to face forward, arms by your sides. On three, and try not to move a muscle.' He tapped the keyboard. 'One … two … three.' When he hit the ENTER key, the booth lit up as horizontal blue beams of light blazed from the bottom of each of its four panels. The beams moved in unison upward as they scanned the full length of Modeen's body.

'Keep your eyes open,' he called. 'Don't worry, you won't go blind.' When the scanner reached the top of the booth, the beams dimmed and the scanning unit returned to the bottom. 'You can come out now, Josephine.'

She emerged from the booth to see a three-dimensional image of herself rotating on the computer screen in front of James.

'Now I need to do a fingerprint scan.' He placed a portable touch screen on the table in front of her. 'Left hand on the screen, if you would.' When she complied, he pressed the ENTER key again. The outline turned green and flashed as bright yellow shock waves radiated from each of her fingertips.

'Now you can take a seat in that chair,' and he indicated it. 'Put your right hand on the back of your head for me.' Inserting a tiny metal cylinder into a handpiece, he rose to stand in front of her. 'Sorry, this may sting a little.' Taking hold of her right elbow, he used an alcohol wipe to swab the delicate skin on her inner arm, just below her well-defined bicep. He threw her a wink. 'Nice guns, by the way.' Pressing the nozzle of the handpiece against her skin, he pulled the trigger.

'Ow! What was that?'

'A tracking chip, so we can find you if ever you're in trouble.' He put down the handpiece and unwrapped a sticking plaster, slapping it over the small entry wound. 'You can put your arm down now.' Turning, he picked up a digital camera. 'Only one more thing to do, the ubiquitous mug shot.' He pointed to the wall. 'Stand over there, thanks. This photo is for your ID card, so unlike your passport photo, you can smile if you like.'

After taking the shot, he removed the camera's memory card and inserted it in the front of his computer. When the downloaded image opened on screen, he studied it for a second, then cropped it and dragged it into a NatSec ID template. A printer at the end of the table whirred into life and Modeen watched the finished article emerge from it. Grabbing it off the printer, James loaded the card into a plastic cradle and attached a retractable lanyard.

'Done. Now clip this to your belt.' He handed it to Modeen. 'Your white access card, the one that will get you through the boom gate, lifts and anywhere else you're authorised to go, is underneath your ID. Keep it with you at all times or you won't be able to enter or leave NatSec facilities … or even get into the loos for that matter.'

'Facilities?'

'Yeah, it'll get you in everywhere except Swan

Island and Pine Gap. I believe Ben has you booked to go to the island in a fortnight's time?'

Modeen shrugged. 'If you say so.'

'Right, well here's your new phone.' He handed her a sleek unit in a black leather cover. 'It has facial recognition software, but also requires a password. Press the ON button at the top and look directly at the phone. If it likes your face – and what's not to like,' he grinned, 'it'll display a login screen for you to enter your password.'

Turning on the phone, she held it at arm's length facing her. When a login screen appeared, she glanced at James. 'What's the password?'

'Jbennett109 for now, but you can change it to whatever you want.'

She typed in the password using the on-screen keypad. 'Okay, I'm in.'

'Good.' James took back the phone. 'Now, let me introduce you to this little baby. She has all the functions of a normal smart phone plus a few handy extras. For instance, there are three camera icons – standard, infrared, and heat-sensing.' He tapped an icon and called, 'Lights please.'

One of the guards reached over and switched off the lights. Darkness descended, broken only by the phone's glow. When James held it in front of Modeen, she could see his image on the screen clearly highlighted in a light greenish hue. He did the same with the heat sensing display, and she saw the shape of his body in varying degrees of red. The brightest spots emanated from his body core and head.

'Wow,' she breathed, 'that's cool.'

'Lights.' Blinking when his request was promptly actioned, James went on. 'Now, if you simultaneously press these two buttons on either side....' He demonstrated and two half-inch silver prongs emerged from the top of the phone. '… and continue holding down the buttons for two seconds....' As he spoke, an electrical arc hissed and cracked between the two prongs. '… you release twenty-five thousand volts at two-point-one milliamps. In other words, you got yourself a handy little Taser right here.' As he released the buttons the prongs retracted. 'Just so you know … one of our agents tried it on his leg.' He shook his head. '*Not* a smart move.'

'Thanks for the tip.'

'Now for another handy feature. The chassis of this little beauty is lined with explosive, a souped-up version of C4 with enough charge to kill everyone in this room.' He waggled his eyebrows at her. 'To set the charge, you click on this icon,' and he held the phone so she could see the screen, 'and set the timer.' Lowering the phone, he pointed to the plaster on her arm. 'Your tracking chip serves as a safeguard. The charge won't go off if you're within four metres of the phone. That's the default distance, but you can vary it if you wish. The explosive won't work in our buildings either,' he added wryly. 'Don't want our own weapons used against us.'

After going on to describe other functions of the phone like the range finder, GPS, and a language translation app, he ran through the checklist on his computer. Sitting back, he announced, 'Well, that concludes my part of your induction. Any questions?'

Modeen shook her head.

'Okay then, I'll take you down to Ben's office. He'll give you the royal guided tour.' James smiled warmly at her and rose to his feet. 'If I've done my job properly, your card should open that,' and he pointed to the partly-concealed door Ben had used earlier.

Striding over to that section of wall, Modeen stretched the lanyard from her belt and swiped her card down the frame. The lanyard sprang back and she heard a distinctive clunk.

As the door swung open, she and James stepped into a narrow corridor and he said conversationally, 'There are four levels to our part of the building. Basically, you've got the carpark up top, then this level which houses security, the armoury, gym and some training rooms. There are more training rooms on level two, along with the control room, management offices, admin, and staff facilities. And in the basement you'll find all the computer gear, special ops command briefing room, and the electronics lab, where I normally hang out.'

He paused by the elevator halfway down the corridor. 'As you know, you can only get down to this level via the carpark lift.' Pressing the button beside the lift doors, he said, 'This one will get you down to the next three levels.'

The doors swished open and they were about to step inside when he put a hand on her arm. 'Hang on, before we leave this level, I think we should make sure your access card works at the armoury.' He twitched a thick eyebrow at her. 'I know how you operatives love your toys, so you'll wanna see this.'

Grinning, he led the way past the elevator to where an armed guard stood outside a hefty steel door. At their approach, the guard turned to face them holding his gun across his chest.

Pulling out his own access card, James said to Modeen, 'This is just to demonstrate what yours *shouldn't* do.' Swiping his card against the panel, he nodded when the indicator light flashed red. 'I'm not authorised to enter this room alone. Apparently,' and he threw her a disgruntled look, 'techos don't need weapons.'

Beside them, the guard put a finger to his earpiece, listened briefly and then growled, 'It's all right. O'Neill's just givin' an induction.'

Muttering drily, 'Big Brother, alive and well,' James turned to Modeen. 'So, whenever someone unautho-rised tries to enter the armoury – or any secure room for that matter – the guys in the control room get an alert, which they follow up,' and he jerked his head toward the guard, 'with the on-site muscle. Okay, now let's try your card.'

On swiping it, she saw the indicator flash green and heard heavy-duty locks release. The door popped open a crack and James opened it wider, as inside the room the lights flickered on automatically.

When chilled air heavy with the scent of gun oil escaped into the corridor, Modeen breathed it in. 'Mmm … smells like my kinda place.'

'Right,' James announced, 'we're in.' He flicked the guard a guilty glance. 'I mean … *you're* in, Josephine.'

She stepped into the five metre square, windowless, vault-like chamber, feeling like she was entering a small firearms shop. Low glass cabinets stacked with ammunition lined the walls. Above them rack upon rack held an impressive array of rifles, pistols, and revolvers. In the centre of the room, an A-frame rack bristled with Carl Gustov, RPG-7, and M72 LAW rocket launchers. They dwarfed the fifty cal sniper rifles and Browning 12 gauge automatic shotguns stacked alongside them.

Murmuring, 'Nice,' Modeen felt James come to stand beside her, as the door closed behind them with a weighty metallic thud.

Moving to the glass cabinet, he indicated the thick bound file resting there. 'This is the register. You have to fill it in whenever you take something so it can be replaced ASAP. The form's self-explanatory, but don't forget to note the serial numbers, etcetera.'

She nodded and walked to the far corner, where she'd spied a stack of familiar-looking carry cases. The bottom two held Nemesis Arms Vanquish sniper rifles, and the next two, Glock 17s. Wondering what the stack of thin wooden boxes beside them might contain, she opened the lid of one. A matching pair of stainless steel Walther CCP nine millimetre pistols glistened up at her from the plush red velvet lining, separated by a suppressor and two spare magazines.

She smacked her lips. '*Very* nice indeed.'

Peering over her shoulder, James said brightly, 'Are we shopping?'

'Not today.' She closed the lid.

'Window shopping, then.' He threw her a wink. 'So, we done?'

'Yep.'

'Okay. You'll need to swipe again to get us out of here. Let's hope I got that right too.' He followed her to the door, and she heard him breathe out when the display flashed green on her swipe and the locks released.

She pushed the door open and nodded at the guard as they made their way back down the corridor. This time, when the lift doors opened, they stepped into the elevator and James pressed the button for level two.

Seconds later the doors parted to reveal an open-plan office area. Eight cubicles containing workstations surrounded a central circular garden. Lit by overhead 'grow' lights, the lush garden featured a rock waterfall from which water tumbled restfully.

'The atrium is a compromise for the lack of windows.' James indicated the seating areas laid out around the garden. 'And a popular spot during breaks.' As he led her past the work stations toward the offices on the other side of the room, he pointed to the first door. 'Steve Robson's office. He's Alfa team manager. Beside his is Beta team manager's office, and to the right is Jack Pender's office. Jack's the operations manager, our "big cheese". The other team managers for Charlie, Delta and Echo teams, are based in the state branches.'

They stopped in front of the door marked BEN SMITH and James rapped on it twice. When a deep voice called, 'Come in,' James ushered Modeen into the room. 'Delivering Ms Bennet, chipped, scanned, safe 'n sound.'

Ben looked up from his computer. 'Thanks James, that'll be all.'

CHAPTER NINE

'Take a seat, JD.' As he spoke, Ben stacked the paperwork on his desk into two neat piles and then sat back. 'You've probably guessed it's no coincidence that Spooky and Bugs … I mean,' and he gave a half smile, 'Mr Williams and Mr Peterson … are members of Beta team, my team.'

When Modeen nodded, he threaded his fingers together and regarded her over them. 'Let's face it, we wouldn't be here today if we hadn't worked so well together as a close-knit Special Forces squad.' He sat forward. 'Sure, we copped some flak for having the first female squad member, but none of us ever regretted having you on board. I'm proud of the fact we quickly proved the critics wrong by treating each other as equals, regardless of gender. In the end we were acknowledged as one of the most effective serving SASR units.'

'I'll take that as a compliment, Mr Smith.' She twitched an eyebrow at him.

Acknowledging her use of his alias with a nod, he said, 'That's how it was intended.'

'And I appreciate the opportunity to be part of a team again,' she went on. 'I was feeling a bit flat and restless after eighteen months of security guard work.'

'Understandably.'

'So….' Leaning forward, she rested her forearms on the desk. '... what sort of additional training will I be doing over the next four weeks?'

'While your military background will prove invaluable, you're going to find this work different from what we did in the Army. The tasks you'll be assigned, the roles NatSec will expect you to undertake, the environments and enemies you'll encounter, will all vary considerably. For that reason, your training will include lessons in deportment and grooming, defensive driving, and the latest espionage techniques.'

She frowned. 'Did you say deportment and grooming?'

'Yes, you heard right.' His lips twitched and then firmed again. 'In this job you're not always going to be in camouflage fatigues, or submerged in a swamp breathing through a straw while waiting to take out a nest of insurgents. You'll be expected to work undercover in any type of civilian setting, from a high society ball to a working mine-site to a sleazy nightclub. Of course you'll be given all the support and resources you need.' Seeing her dubious expression, he added, 'There'll also be opportunities for military-type black ops, just ask Spook. He got into some black water on one of his recent missions.'

At her slow nod, Ben sat back in his chair again. 'For now, I think we'll break for lunch. This is your first day after all.' His dark eyes twinkled. 'We have the rest of the afternoon to finish your orientation.' As he got to his feet, she followed suit. Pausing, he said, 'I'm glad you decided to come on board, JD.'

'Glad you invited me, Ben.' They shared a smile and she asked, 'Hey, James said something about me going to Swan Island?'

'Yes, you'll be spending a couple of days there, learning to do some MacGyver stuff.' He grinned at her bemused expression. 'You know, like making a bomb out of a shoestring and a piece of bubble gum.'

She arched an amused eyebrow at him.

'Oh, and you'll need these.' He reached into the top drawer and pulled out a set of car keys, tossing them to her.

She caught them and quipped, 'These won't explode, will they?'

'You catch on quick.' He grinned again. 'I'll give you the run-down later. Now, let's get outta here.' He led the way out and past the operations manager's office. As they rounded the solid floor-to-ceiling partition that circled the central garden, he announced, 'This is the kitchen and dining area.'

Modeen stopped abruptly, taken aback by the crowd gathered around a large table spread with food. At her arrival, all conversation stopped and they stood eyeing her with open curiosity.

'A little welcome-aboard gathering for you,' Ben explained as he strode into the room, where he addressed the group. 'I'd like you all to meet Josephine Bennet, our new addition to Beta team.' There was a ripple of applause and calls of, 'G'day Jo,' and, 'Welcome to NatSec,' and then Ben turned to Modeen. 'I'll introduce you to the crew.' Seeing a tall, distinguished-looking older man step forward, Ben bent his head and murmured, 'Nothing like starting at the top.' Raising his head again he said, 'JD, this is operations manager, Jack Pender.'

Eyeing her shrewdly, Jack extended a hand. 'I've read your brief, Josephine, very impressive. It's good to have you on board.'

She returned his firm handshake. 'Thank you, Jack. It's good to be here.'

Ben moved her on to the next person. 'And this is our resource manager, Leanne Martin.'

'Nice to meet you, Josephine.' The sharp-eyed, well-dressed woman shook Modeen's hand and then Ben introduced a group of four staffers. 'You've already met resident techie James,' who threw her a wink. 'With him is computer tech Harper Johnson, logistics officer Reece Riley, and Bryan Harris. Bryan handles intel.'

They all shook Modeen's hand as Ben continued. 'Hot drinks, etcetera, are over here, and the rest rooms are through there.' He pointed to a door to the right of the kitchen area. 'After lunch, I've asked Harper to assign you a cubicle to use whenever you're here in HQ. She'll show you the ropes and issue your comms equipment. I've also asked her to give you a tour of the basement level briefing room and computer lab. When you've finished, come back up to my office and collect your duffel. I'll have your accommodation details ready by then.' Seeing Jack beckoning from the other end of the table, Ben said, 'If you'll excuse me,' and strode over to join his boss.

Bryan Harris sidled up to Modeen. 'So, Josephine, welcome to the team.' He was surprisingly softly-spoken for a big man.

She turned to him with a smile. 'Thanks Bryan.'

'Say, I believe you were asking Ben about your old squad member, Eric Crockman?'

Her eyes took on a more serious slant. 'I was, yes.'

'Ben asked me to look into the circumstances of Crockman's MIA. I'm afraid I haven't been able to uncover any new details about the incident. It occurred in a politically sensitive hotspot, as did most of your operations, so his body was never recovered nor his death verified. The Army released the usual BS they use when they don't want it known our troops were in a certain vicinity.' He gazed earnestly at her. 'That's all I know at this stage, sorry.'

She met his gaze. 'Thanks anyway, Bryan. I'd only recently heard Gator – that's what we called Eric,' and she gave a quick smile, 'was missing in action. And then my curiosity was aroused when a bloke told me he'd seen Gator in Sydney about two months ago.' She shook her head. 'I guess he was mistaken.'

'Well, Crockman's personal bank account hasn't been touched, so I'd say it's highly unlikely he made it back to Oz … if he's still alive.' Bryan rubbed his chin. 'I was surprised to see how much debt he was in before his last mission. Were you and he close?'

She shrugged a shoulder. 'Not overly. We had a good rapport though, and I would've liked us to have caught up once we were both civilians.'

'Josephine, come and grab some tucker.' Harper came to stand beside them. 'They've laid on a good spread for you and the seagulls have swooped.' She indicated the rapidly diminishing food on the table. 'After you've eaten I'll take you down to meet your new laptop.'

'Thanks, Harper. And call me Jo.'

'Right, Jo.' The fresh-faced young woman smiled warmly at her. 'I was just about to make a coffee for myself, can I make one for you too?'

'Thanks. White with one.'

As Harper made her way to the kitchen counter, Modeen heard a cheery voice behind her say, 'Hope you're enjoying this little gathering in your honour, Josephine.'

She turned to see Leanne and Reece smiling at her. She returned their smiles, saying, 'Please, call me Jo. Only Mum calls me Josephine.'

'Jo it is.' Leanne gave a polite dip of her head. 'As resource manager and logistics officer,' and she indicated the lean young man at her side, 'Reece and I work together. So if there's anything you need just ring either one of us and we'll organise it for you. We're also your next best contact if you can't reach Ben. In situations where you find yourself detained or obstructed by the authorities, we can help out.'

Modeen nodded. 'Does that happen often?'

Reece stepped forward to answer. 'Not really, but it's better to call us than to … um … resort to other methods, like busting heads or shooting your way out.' His expression grew pained. 'We like to keep things off the evening news if we can.'

Modeen gave an amused snort and murmured, 'Wolf.'

'Excuse me?' Leanne was gazing at her curiously.

'Nothing, just … what Reece described then made me think of Troy Wolverton, a friend of mine.'

Leanne looked over at Reece. 'AKA Troy Ryan?' At his nod, she turned back to Modeen. 'You two know each other?'

Making a mental note of Wolf's alias, Modeen replied, 'Yes, and you get to know someone pretty well when you've crawled through a swamp on your bellies together.'

'Of course, you were both in the military.' As she spoke, Leanne noticed Jack beckoning them. She murmured, "Scuse us,' and they hurried away just as Harper placed a steaming cup in front of Modeen.

'Here's your coffee, Jo.'

'Thanks. So, how long have you worked here?'

'Nearly two years now,' the young woman said shyly. 'I had just completed an IT degree through Monash University when the next thing I knew, I was being head-hunted, by James.' She took a sip from her cup and mumbled, 'I'm lucky, he's a good boss. Has been showing me the ropes ever since.'

'Not that I needed to show her much,' James interjected from behind them. 'She graduated with honours, and is an excellent worker.' He turned to Modeen. 'How's the arm? Not too sore, I hope?'

'Nah, feels pretty good.' She flexed her bicep.

His eyes widened and he swallowed. 'Great.' Pushing his glasses further up his nose, he turned to glance at the remnants of food on the table. 'Just one more morsel, then I'd better get back to work.'

Following Harper into a dimly-lit computer lab on the basement level, Modeen took in the hundreds of blinking LEDs and the walls lined with computer cabinets stacked full of the latest fibre-optic routers, modems, and switch panels. A black IBM Power9 server and system storage unit filled one whole corner of the room. It hummed with raw, caged energy.

Modeen indicated the gear with a sweep of her arm. 'A bit over the top for the number of staff here, isn't it?'

'Oh, it's not just for us,' Harper replied. 'ASIO shares our system, and we're linked in with Swan Island and the Pine Gap facility.' Heading toward a cluttered desk, she dug a tablet out from under a jumble of computer print-outs, LAN cables, and mother boards. She handed the tablet to Modeen and pointed at a laptop. 'That's yours too.'

Modeen glanced at the displays. Both contained the familiar verification hand outline.

'Other authorised NatSec agents can login to your computer and tablet,' Harper went on, 'but can only access their own files, not any of your information. The same goes for you with their laptops.'

Modeen nodded her understanding. 'I do have some IT experience. As a signaller in the SASR I was responsible for comms, which encompassed Electronic Warfare, COMSEC, and even Morse code.'

Harper stopped what she was doing and glanced at Modeen. 'Machine code, did you say?'

'Machine code?'

'You know, all the ones and zeros.'

Modeen shook her head. '*Morse* code, all the dots and dashes.' She grinned. 'Older but not quite as out-dated as Machine code.'

'Oh … right.' With a quick, bemused frown, Harper carried on. 'Anyway, we use the latest broadband technology and security, with super-fast wireless for remote connections. You can seamlessly synchronise your devices with our network for the latest updates.' Reaching down, she plucked a bright puce-pink Post-it note off her desk. 'Now, for your NatSec email address.' She read from the note, spelling out, '… jbennet at NatSec dot org dot au,' and then handed the note to Modeen. 'Your password is the same one you use for your phone. Whenever you change either your email or phone password, the other will update automatically.'

After watching Modeen log into the tablet and computer to verify her email login details, she said brightly, 'Right, now for that tour of the electronics lab and command briefing room.' She indicated the tablet and laptop. 'You can leave that gear here if you like.'

As they headed out of the computer lab and down the corridor, Harper stopped outside a large set of double glass doors in a wall made entirely of glass. 'This is the special ops command briefing room. It's mostly used by the operations and team managers when planning missions, so this is where it all happens. Agents seldom sit in, unless they're heavily involved in a case … and available. Because they're based off-site, agents – and that means you,' and she threw Modeen a smile, 'usually receive instructions via email or phone.' Her expression grew thoughtful.

'That's about all I can tell you about this room, haven't spent any time in it myself. I've only ever been called into it once to fix a technical problem with the Wi-Fi connection.'

As Modeen peered through the doors into the room, Harper said, 'Once the doors close the room is sealed. It feels like you're under a cone of silence. There's also a switch you can flick to make the doors and the whole glass wall opaque. It's really cool, secret squirrel-type stuff. No one outside the room can see or hear anything.' She paused and frowned. 'I guess we're better off not knowing what's discussed in here.'

'I think you'd sleep better at night,' Modeen murmured, and then gave her a reassuring smile. 'Is that it for now?' At Harper's nod, she said, 'Thanks for the tour. I can find my own way back to Ben's office. I'll have a play with the tablet and computer tonight, and come and see you tomorrow if I have any problems.'

'Cheers, Jo.'

Modeen rapped on the door, and heard Ben call, 'Come in.'

When she stepped into his office, he looked up and then sat back in his chair. 'So, how's your first day been? Brain about to overload?'

She gave an amused huff. 'Nah, all good. And you've got a great bunch of people working here.'

'I think they were impressed with you too. Now,'

and he handed her a printed page, 'here are your reservation details. I've booked you into the Rydges Hotel just around the corner.' Rising, he collected her duffel from the floor. 'I think that'll do for your first day. C'mon, I'll walk you out.'

Back on level one, they passed through security and entered the elevator, which carried them smoothly to the carpark level. Stepping out of the lift, Ben called over his shoulder, 'You got those car keys?' as he headed toward one of the Aurions.

Reaching into her pocket, Modeen pulled out the key ring he had given her earlier and tossed it to him. It contained a typical-looking remote control unit with a built-in retractable key and three buttons: LOCK, OPEN and TRUNK.

Ben laid the unit flat in the palm of his hand. 'See this indentation? There's one on the other side as well. If you press both down at the same time, the back of the remote comes off.' He demonstrated. 'That's like pulling the pin on a grenade. Now all you need to do is press the LOCK button. When the red light starts flashing, you've got five seconds before it blows. Make sure you throw it well away from yourself. It's got enough charge to lift a small car off the ground.'

After carefully reassembling the unit, he pressed the button to open the car's trunk. 'Once back together, the explosive function disarms and the unit's just your run-of-the-mill car remote again.' He tossed the keys back to her. 'Now, did Spooky run you through the contents of the boot?'

'As a matter of fact, he did.' Modeen leaned forward and lifted the floor panel. Seeing what lay beneath it, she turned to beam at him. 'You remembered.'

As in Spooky's car, there was an MP5SD6 and a sniper rifle, but a brand new Walther PPX and silencer sat in place of the Glock 17.

Ben patted her shoulder. 'We can't have you going on a mission without your mate, Walt.' He replaced the cover, closed the trunk, and pointed past the black 4WDs to the far side of the basement. 'The exit ramp is through that roller door. Just swipe your card to get out. Or, if you're walking, you can use the stairs. They'll take you out to the street in front of the building. Rydges is only two blocks down.'

'Thanks Ben, think I'll take the stairs. Could use the exercise.'

'Right.' He handed over her duffel. 'See you tomorrow at o-eight hundred. First up you've got a self-defence lesson.'

After watching him stride back to the elevator, she walked to the door marked STAIRS and swiped her card. The light on the wall panel flashed green and the heavy steel door unlocked with a mechanical clunk. Pulling it open, she climbed the stairs and stepped out into the street, wrapping her coat tighter against Melbourne's afternoon chill.

CHAPTER TEN

Heading to the gym on level one of the NatSec building the next morning, Modeen found two other agents already in judo suits leaning against the wall. They were watching a tall, dark-skinned instructor lay out thick blue mats in the centre of the gym. At her approach, they straightened and the nearest one extended a hand.

'G'day. I'm Craig.' He indicated the sandy-haired young man beside him. 'And this is Wyatt.'

'Jo.'

Regarding her intently as they all shook hands, Craig said, 'We're with Charlie team, both ex-detectives. What about you?'

'Beta team, and I'm ex-SASR.'

'Wow,' Wyatt piped up, 'I didn't think they had women in the Special Forces?'

'Yeah … I hear that a lot.' She sighed. 'I was the first to be accepted.'

'Well done you.'

'Hi guys.' The American accent belonged to the instructor, who'd finished laying out the mats to make a six by seven metre pad. He walked up to them tightening the belt on his black judo suit, his movements easy, his six foot four physique strong yet supple. Handing Modeen a judo suit and belt, he said, 'We're just waitin' for one more person to arrive. When you've changed, please take a seat along the edge of the mat.'

Emerging from the change room a few minutes later, she stopped in her tracks on seeing another man stride into the gym. Obviously the instructor's one more person, he was tall, brawny, dark-haired, and grizzled-looking. A real rough-nut type.

And very familiar….

She watched him being greeted by the instructor, who also handed him a jacket and belt. Without a glance at the other three, the new arrival made his way to the change room. When he emerged a few minutes later, he strode to the mat and folded his long muscular frame to sit cross-legged beside Modeen.

Running her eyes over his strong countenance with its dark brows, sharp, hooded eyes, and the once-handsome nose now crooked after a bungled reset, her lips parted in a broad smile. 'How're you going, Wolf?'

Still gazing ahead, he said, 'Not bad, Modeen.' His voice was even more gravelly than she remembered.

When he finally turned to meet her gaze, they fist-bumped and his mouth tipped upward in one corner. Nudging her slender shoulder with his brawny one, he drawled, 'You're lookin' as fit as ever.'

In the centre of the mat, the instructor clapped his hands. 'Right, everyone. I'm Leroy Armstrong, your self-defence instructor. To give you a bit of back-ground, I'm experienced in Judo, Karate, Kung Fu and Ju-Jitsu. I'll start each session with a brief explanation of the core principles behind each of these disciplines. First, Judo.' He moved slowly around the mat rubbing his hands together.

'Judo was founded by Jigoro Kano and is funda-mentally about *kuzushi*, which means disturbin' the balance of your opponent, usin' their weight and momentum against them.' He beckoned for Modeen to come forward, saying, 'I will give a demonstration of balance.' When she joined him in the centre of the mat, he planted his feet, shoulder-width apart. 'Now, young lady, try and push me off balance.'

She took a wide stance and shoved hard against his broad chest. He didn't budge. She went behind him and shoved even harder against his taut back. Again, he didn't shift from his position.

'As you can see,' he said coolly, 'when your oppo-nent is firmly grounded, it's hard to move him, espe-cially for a smaller challenger. Hard … but not impossible, if you employ the right technique. Timin' is important to get someone off balance. For example, if I take a step forward, I only have one foot on the ground mid-stride. At that point, I could be easily pushed off balance by a shove from an opponent.'

With a nod to Modeen, he began walking slowly past her. She timed his steps and as he raised his right foot, she shoved his left shoulder.

Stumbling sideways and then righting himself, he bowed to her. 'Very good.' Still facing her, he planted his feet on the mat as before. 'Now, try to push me again.'

This time, when she moved in to shove him in the chest, he caught her wrist, stepped sideways, and jerked her arm past him, sending her stumbling forward. Throwing her arms down, she tucked her head and rolled, and in one smooth motion was back on her feet, facing him.

'Well done. You've obviously had some trainin'.' He dipped his head again and turned to the others. 'If you use your opponent's momentum against him … or her … there is very little they can do about it.' Facing Modeen and once more planting himself on the mat, he ordered, 'Again.'

This time when he grabbed her wrist and stepped sideways, she reversed his hold, grasped his arm, and used her own momentum to swing up and behind him. Reaching around his neck, she took hold of the opposite lapel of his judo jacket, yanking it backward.

Caught off guard, he lessened his grip on her wrist and she whipped her hand out of his grasp. Seizing the opposite lapel, she pulled it tight and he dropped to his knees, gasping for breath. She increased the pressure on the stranglehold until he tapped the side of his leg twice to signal submission. Releasing him, Modeen backed away while he remained on his knees, coughing and rubbing his neck.

At the edge of the mat, Craig and Wyatt shared a glance and then turned to Wolf, who merely shrugged.

With a sheepish glance at his audience, Leroy spluttered, 'Most important lesson … never underestimate … your opponent.' Rising to his feet, he shared a bow with Modeen and addressed the group again. 'While strangleholds are seldom used in Judo, we will cover them in more depth when we move on to the Ju-Jitsu part of the presentation. I will also go over wrist-locks and the use of weapons. Of course in a street fight, it is best to use a combination of martial art disciplines. Your strategy will depend on the number, size, and strength of your opponents.'

He lifted his chin at Modeen. 'You have some skills. Would you like to share with us the details of your trainin'?'

'Um … okay.' She stepped forward. 'In the Army I received basic self-defence training, and I also have some Judo and Ju-Jitsu experience. Most of my martial arts training has been in Filipino Kali.' She warmed to her subject. 'I'm also a fan of Jeet Kune Do, though I mostly use martial arts as a last resort. At close quarters, I find my Walther PPX to be the best defence.'

Swallowing a grin, Leroy bowed again and gestured for her to take a seat. 'That's a good point.' He eyed the group. 'Fair fights are for tournaments and gradings. In a real life or death situation, there are no prizes for second best. So if you have any sort of advantage, use it.'

The students nodded their understanding.

'Now, before we get into some moves, it's important you know how to fall in case you're on the receivin' end of a foot sweep or throw. As our student demonstrated earlier, if you can roll and get to your feet again quickly to face your opponent, there's less chance of being compromised,' and he gestured for them to get up.

'Enthusiasm … that's what I like to see.' Grinning, he slapped his hands together. 'You'll be pleased to know I've been booked to give you lessons every mornin' this week. Tomorrow we'll be coverin' Ju-Jitsu, startin' at eight am sharp. Please bring your judogi with you.' He tugged the lapels of his jacket. 'For now, I want you to pair off. We're gonna try some recoveries, forward rolls, break falls, foot sweeps, and throws.'

After the class ended, Modeen rose to her feet and nudged Wolf. 'Got time for a cuppa?'

'Yeah, but I've got another class in forty minutes.'

His expression soured. 'Apparently I need to learn how to look and act like a gentleman.'

Grinning, she said, 'You think *you're* hard done-by? I've got deportment and grooming lessons next.'

He gave a bark of laughter and shook his head. 'What the hell have we signed up for? At least in the Army they didn't care what we said or how we were dressed before we whacked someone.'

Still grinning, she said, 'Come on, let's get that drink,' and turned to Craig and Wyatt. 'What about you guys, wanna join us for a coffee?'

Wyatt smiled. 'Thanks, but we've gotta get over to Swan Island.'

'No worries. Have fun.'

In the kitchen on level two, Modeen dug out two mugs. 'Still black coffee, no sugar?' At his nod, she poured the boiling water and then brought their cups to the table. Setting Wolf's in front of him, she said idly, 'So, you been up to anything interesting lately?'

'Well....' He took a tentative sip from his mug, blinking his dark eyes in the rising steam, and then threw her a glance. 'You know we're not supposed to discuss our missions with anyone, including other agents? Unless they're on the same assignment, of course.'

'Oh ... I didn't know that. Makes sense I guess.'

'Anyway, I've been on half a dozen or so missions since joining, and they've been pretty straightfor-ward.' Putting down his mug, he rubbed a hand over his darkly stubbled chin, making a rasping sound. 'The hardest thing I've found after leaving the service is goin' back to thinkin' like a civilian. Seems like Ben and Spooky might've managed it, but I'm still workin' on it.' As he spoke, his thick black brows drew together. 'Takin' more time than I thought it would.'

Modeen gave a solemn nod over the rim of her mug.

'Anyway,' he went on, 'I'm with Delta team and based in Western Australia. I'm just here for some refresher trainin'.' His face darkened. 'Mind you, nobody said anythin' about havin' etiquette lessons from a weedy lookin' frog called Pierre LeMar.' With a bemused huff, he raised his eyebrows at Modeen. *Eti-quette*, can you believe it?' He sighed. 'This is more up Spooky's alley. He's comfortable wearin' suits.'

Sitting forward, she put a hand on his arm. 'I'm sure you'll do fine. And Spooky's still the same bloke, just adapting faster.' She sat back again. 'You'd still want him on your side, wouldn't you?'

'Of course. Don't get me wrong, when the chips are down that guy's a weapon.'

'He sure is.'

They shared a grin and then Wolf said resignedly, 'Anyway, I guess my lack of finesse is why they've got me doin' this trainin'.'

'Reckon the same goes for me.' She threw him a rueful glance.

Gazing at her a moment, he said gruffly, 'You heard about Gator?'

She lowered her eyes. 'Only that he's missing in action.' Looking up again, she said, 'You know … someone thought they might've seen him in Sydney about two months ago.'

'Really?' Wolf gave a speculative frown.

'He must've been mistaken, though,' Modeen went on. 'We would've heard from Gator otherwise.'

'Yeah, we would'a been the first to know if he'd made it back.' Watching her drain the last of her coffee, Wolf shook his head. 'We could'a used him here, that's for sure. He's talented, especially with explosives … and a good mate,' and he threw her a knowing glance.

She nodded, her eyes once more fixed on the table.

'Do you recall the mission when we stormed that Taliban stronghold?' Wolf went on. 'Ben gave Gator the Barrett sniper rifle so he could cover us from the hillside, remember?'

'How could I forget? He took out the mongrel who gave me this,' and she rubbed the scar on her left shoulder.

'Well … in the "mongrel's" defence, you and Walt *were* havin' a close quarters party with four of his mates.' He threw her a lopsided grin. 'And you were lucky, the bullet went clean through without shattering bone.' He sobered. 'If it wasn't for Gator, I don't reckon you or I would be here. For a powder monkey he pulled off some pretty amazin' shots that day. Eight kills, all head shots, over twelve hundred metres.' Wolf gave a drawn-out whistle. 'I started worryin' I might be replaced as squad sniper.'

'Yeah … well, I thought about it.' The deep voice came from behind them. They turned to see Ben stroll into the room. 'Then I realised that might've meant making you our powder monkey,' and he gave a mock-grimace. 'I didn't fancy having us all blown to the smithereens.' At Wolf's offended expression, he slapped him on the back. 'Just kiddin', mate.' Grabbing a mug from the shelf, he added, 'Anyway, we all knew our way around a fifty cal. Let's face it, if we couldn't shoot, we wouldn't have been in the Special Forces.'

At their murmurs of agreement, he enquired, 'So, ready for your next lesson?' When they stared at him without answering, he stared back at them with a knowing gleam in his eyes. 'I think you'll find it inter-esting as well as beneficial.'

Wolf merely scowled, as Modeen muttered, 'If you say so,' and winced. 'I can't *wait* to meet …,' and she put on a French accent, '… *la belle dame Vivienne DeMarschelier.*'

Ben glanced at her in surprise. *'Parlez-vous Français?'*

She gave a bark of laughter. 'No! Just picked up a few words here and there. Hey, but what about you?'

'Taking lessons.' Ben shifted his feet awkwardly and then straightened. 'Anyway, let me know how you get on.'

'Will do. And now we'd better get our skates … er … stilettos on.' She rolled her eyes and the two men grinned.

The three of them left the kitchen together. Ben headed to his office, half-finished mug of coffee in hand, while Modeen and Wolf made their way along the corridor toward the training rooms.

As soon as they were out of Ben's earshot, Wolf whispered, 'Was he speakin' French?'

She nodded. 'If he's taking lessons he must need to speak it for some reason. A mission maybe?'

Wolf grunted. 'Yeah, maybe. I just hope that doesn't mean *we'll* have to learn other languages,' and he gave a contemptuous sniff.

'It's probably on the cards,' she said drily, 'like just about everything else. Now, which room are you in?'

'Two.'

'I'm in three.'

When they reached the doorway marked TRAINING ROOM 2, Wolf stopped to murmur darkly but with a gleam in his eyes, 'Wish me luck.'

'What for?'

'I'm gonna need it, and all the patience I can muster, to keep from squashin' the frog.' Raising an eyebrow at her stifled laugh, he strode through the door.

CHAPTER ELEVEN

Gazing at the file in her hands, the woman murmured, *'Intéressant ...,'* and flicked a manicured hand to indicate the chair in front of a desk. 'Take a seat, *s'il vous plaît.'*

As she approached the desk, Modeen ran her eyes over its contents. The engraved silver pen resting in a pewter holder was the most businesslike item. In place of the usual paperwork, computer equipment and stationery, a stylish glass vase of white and red roses sat alongside a collection of professionally-shot photographs in silver frames. Her nose caught the scent of French perfume and she once more eyed the poised woman standing in front of her, oozing panache in her tailored linen suit and carefully coiffured hair.

Finding herself wondering if there were a strand rebellious enough to escape the flawless chignon,

Modeen said mildly, 'So, you're an image consultant. What does that entail?'

After gliding past her and behind the desk, the woman dropped gracefully into her chair and removed a photo from the file, putting it face-up in front of Modeen. Glancing down at it, she saw first the dense foliage and then the well-camouflaged soldier amid the undergrowth. A barely visible presence in full tactical gear, face roughly streaked at forty-five degree angles in brown and green paint, the soldier was peering down the sights of an M4 Carbine assault rifle.

The consultant raised her expertly made-up eyes to gaze into Modeen's face. Pointing a crimson-tipped finger at the picture, she said in a heavy French accent, '*Dîtes-moi,* is this you?'

Leaning forward, Modeen glanced at the picture again and nodded. 'Think that was East Timor.'

The woman put the picture back in the file. '*Je vois.* Then it is obvious you grasp *l'idée* of blending in.'

'You didn't answer my question, Ma'am.'

The woman sighed and arched a sculptured eyebrow. 'To blend in, one must project the right image. That is where I come in. My name is Vivienne DeMarschelier, and what we will be working on is applying your *compétences de camouflage* to situations other than jungle warfare.'

Modeen extended a hand. 'And I'm Josephine … Bennet.' She almost forgot to use her alias. When, after a moment's hesitation, Vivienne gave her outstretched hand a limp shake, Modeen swallowed a look of distaste and withdrew her hand as soon as was polite. 'Tell me, what sort of situations are you talking about?'

'*Disons que ...,*' and Vivienne tapped her chin with a dainty fingertip, '... you are escorting a male agent to *une réception,* say ... a cocktail party *diplomatique.* You cannot both be in dinner suits.' She gave an elegant shrug of one shoulder. 'You will need to blend in with all the other sophisticated male and female *dignitaires* there. You must not stand out, so you will not be wearing *this,*' and she indicated Modeen's shirt and jeans with a disdainful flick of a finger. '*Non, non, non!* You will be wearing an evening gown and *les bijoux,* the jewellery. Your makeup and hair will be impeccable, you will be a picture of *élégance.* For *that* mission.'

She paused. 'But for the next assignment, you are *une serveuse,* a waitress. You will be dressed as such, and made-up to look like the girl next door, *non?* And when required to visit a sleazy nightclub as a *patron,* you will be dressed accordingly. Tight, revealing clothing, dark heavy makeup, *et ... peut-être ...,*' and her tone fell as she said with distaste, '... you will be chewing gum. *Vous comprennez ...* you understand?'

Modeen gave a slow, uncertain nod as Vivienne rose to her feet.

'Now, let us get started, *oui?*' Putting an elegant finger on top of Modeen's head, she walked around her, looking her over. 'You are *belle,* beautiful, underneath ...,' and her glossed lips turned downward, '...

all this *manly* clothing. But being beautiful in the kind of business you are in, can be an advantage … or *problème*. And these we must be able both to use, and to overcome.'

She stood back and crossed her arms. 'Behind that door, you will find *la rendez-robe*, the wardrobe. Let us imagine you are going undercover to the high-class cocktail party we spoke of. You will go into that room and choose an outfit you think would be suitable for *l'occasion*. You may use whatever you like, but remember, you need to blend in.'

Modeen rose to her feet, staring at her sceptically. 'So … you want me to dress-up.'

Vivienne gave a dramatic roll of eyes. 'I want you to blend into *les environs* I have described to you, as you did in the jungle.'

'O … kay.' Turning, Modeen made her way to the room. Inside, she found rows of gowns and various other outfits in a range of sizes, along with wigs, shoes, and makeup. Sighing, she flipped through the evening gowns and selected an off-the-shoulder shift in peacock-blue chiffon over satin.

Stripping off her shirt and jeans, she slipped the gown over her head. Like a peacock-blue cloud it floated downward to settle softly on her firm curves. After a quick scan of the shoe selection, she chose a low-heeled pair of silver sandals. Next, she took a long, auburn wig from off the shelf and pulled it over her short hair. Seating herself in front of the mirror, she began applying makeup, until the person staring back at her looked very little like the fresh-faced woman who'd entered the room.

Spying a tray of French perfumes, she sniffed a few until she found one she liked. Holding the bottle away from herself, she sprayed a mist of fragrance and walked through it on her way out of the room.

On her approach, Vivienne raked her with critical eyes. Twirling a finger, she commanded, 'Walk to the end of the room, *s'il vous plaît*, and then pirouette and walk back to me. Do it *doucement*, slowly.' When Modeen obliged, Vivienne clapped her hands. *'Bravo!* You are light on your feet, have a lovely figure, and striking features.' She sniffed the air delicately. 'And you found the fragrances, good.' Smiling for the first time, she moved to stand in front of Modeen, taking her face between both hands. 'Hmm … china blue eyes. We will need to alter the colour from time to time.' She gave a dismissive shrug. 'This is not a *problème*, we have the contact lenses.'

Turning Modeen's face to the right, she murmured, 'High cheek bones, and a *beau* complexion,' and then ushered her to the full-length mirror in a corner of the room. 'You are tall and slim, although *un peu* muscular….' She touched a finger to one of Modeen's well-formed biceps and shrugged. 'But this is easy to hide, not so easy to create.'

Taking a step back, she announced, 'Now we must see what does *not* work. Ah, yes. First, we start beneath the gown. Its sheer, fitted outline calls for invisible lingerie, *non?* Victoria's Secret, *naturellement.'* She sniffed. *'Le string,* what you call G-string. And not this … what you call … sports bra.'

Modeen glanced down at the gown's plunging neckline and pulled a face. Her practical and decidedly non-racy bra was clearly visible, peeking out of the deep vee.

'Now, the shoes.' Vivienne flicked a contemptuous hand at them. 'These are all wrong. They might be comfortable, but they are *not* what one wears with this kind of gown. Nor to this type of *occasion.* I will find you a better pair while you remove that *brassière.'* At Modeen's puzzled expression, she sighed. 'I want to see if you can go *sans brassière* in this type of dress.'

When Modeen made to move, Vivienne raised a hand. *'Mais … un moment.'* Stepping closer, she pulled a powdered rouge from out of a pocket. After dipping a small brush into it, she applied the powder to Modeen's cheeks in swift, light strokes. Stepping back to examine her handiwork, she said, *'Oui,* that is much better. If one has high cheekbones, one must draw attention to them.'

She ran her eyes over the rest of Modeen's face and pressed her lips together. 'We will try a *différente* shade of lipstick next time, one of *my* choosing.' Flapping a hand, she ordered, 'Now go.' At Modeen's long-suffering sigh, she snapped, 'Spare me the affectations of martyrdom, *ma chère*. This is all part of your training.'

When she once more emerged from the change room, Modeen found Vivienne holding out two pairs of patent, skin-coloured court shoes. One pair had high stiletto heels, the other pointed but lower heels.

After eyeing her shrewdly, Vivienne put down the high-heeled versions. 'With your height, you do not need these. We cannot have you *imposante*, towering over everyone. Otherwise you will not blend in.' She handed Modeen the medium-heeled courts. 'These should be your size.'

Modeen slipped them on.

'Now, let me see you....' Taking a step back, Vivienne looked Modeen up and down. '*Oui, parfait*. With your firm physique, you do not need a *brassiére* with a gown like that. And I see you have removed your briefs. *Bon* improvisation.' She frowned. 'How old are you, *ma chère?* Twenty-four? Twenty-five?'

'Twenty-eight.'

'*Mon dieu!* It is not often I am wrong when guessing a woman's age. *Je suis impressionee!* With the right outfit and makeup you could pass for much younger.'

'Thank you ... I think.'

'Now, show me how you walk in the shoes.' At Modeen's first unsteady steps, Vivienne muttered, 'Hmm ... some deportment lessons *peut-être*.'

'I'm not used to wearing heels.'

'*Oui*, this I can see. You will need to practice so as to

look poised and confident when wearing them.' Putting both hands on Modeen's shoulders, she turned her full circle, raking her with eagle eyes. Stepping back, she clicked her tongue. 'You have exquisite skin, it is a shame about the blemishes,' and she indicated the slight indentation on Modeen's cheek.

Moving closer, she examined the small area of puckered skin on the front of Modeen's shoulder. After running a fingertip over the exit wound's larger, raised scar near her shoulder blade, Vivienne pursed her lips and said tightly, 'This is not so good. The smaller blemishes can be easily concealed with foundation, however *ce défaut* on your shoulder blade will be much harder to hide. Of course it is not so *répugnant* that it detracts from your beauty, but it is something that is easily recognisable.'

She stepped back and clasped her hands together. 'No matter. This is *simplement un petit détail* we will consider when selecting your gowns. And now, we will try another … what you call … dress-up, for a very *différente* situation.'

CHAPTER TWELVE

Ben put down the phone and rose to his feet, stretching his tall frame and wishing his job entailed more fieldwork and less time at a desk. Glad of the opportunity to stretch his legs, he stepped out of his office, in time to see Reece jog along the corridor ahead of him and then duck into the control room.

Ben frowned.

Was something amiss?

He moved quietly along the corridor and stopped to listen outside the control room.

Something was definitely amiss.

Keeping his movements stealthy, he entered the room. Once his eyes adjusted to the lower lighting, he spotted Reece and three of the security guards huddled over one of the many security monitors. Oblivious to his arrival, they continued staring at the screen, giving occasional whistles and sniggers.

What could be so entertaining about security footage?

Ben moved closer to look over their shoulders at the screen. He took a double take at the sight of two women, one in a suit and neat chignon, and the other in skin-tight black pants, knee-high stiletto boots, gleaming black leather bodice, and a raven-haired bob. When she turned toward the camera, all five men sucked in a breath. Her heavy, dark makeup made Modeen look both menacing … and exotic.

At Ben's roared, 'What the hell?' the four voyeurs jumped, and the seated guard hastily reached forward to switch off the monitor.

When Reece made to scuttle past him, Ben barred the way with a brawny, tattooed arm. 'I don't have time to deal with this now,' he growled, 'but the five of us will be talking about this improper use of company resources and invasion of privacy, later.' He glowered at Reece and then each of the others in turn. 'In the meantime, I want you to think about the disrespect you've shown to a professional colleague who was simply undertaking assigned training.'

Dropping his arm he barked, 'Now get back to work, all of you.' Turning on his heel, he marched stiff-backed from the room, doing his best to suppress a grin. After making his way to the special ops command briefing room, he found Jack Pender waiting for him.

Jack greeted him with a nod. 'Close the door would you, Ben?'

As he did so, Ben flicked a switch and the doors and front wall of the room turned from clear glass to opaque.

'Remember this guy?' Jack indicated a large LCD screen mounted on the wall.

Peering at the image of a squat, swarthy man, Ben muttered, 'Salvatore Batista. Sydney-based black marketeer, low-level mobster and brothel owner. Ambitious, power-hungry, with delusions of prominence.'

Jack nodded and said grimly, 'And we've just received some more, rather troubling info. It links him to an attempted aircraft hijacking in the US.'

'Hijacking?' Ben frowned. 'Must've been a recent attempt, otherwise I would've heard about it.'

'The Yanks are keeping the incident under wraps for now. Luckily, the attempt was foiled before it became another nine-eleven. The geniuses involved boarded a seven-forty-seven out of Vancouver, and managed – by mistake I assume – to seat themselves next to a group of CIA agents returning to Washington. One of the agents thought the perps looked nervous, so he quizzed them. When their stories didn't match, they were arrested and taken back to base. They spilled their guts at the grilling, and named Batista as a major player.'

Ben's lips tightened and he shook his head.

'It appears Batista's been taking regular sorties to Khartoum in the Sudan and Mogadishu in Somalia,'

Jack went on. 'It's believed he's become associated with a splinter group of one of the larger terrorist organisations.' Pressing a button, he pulled up another photograph.

It showed Batista standing in a littered alleyway with three armed men at his sides and back, and four standing facing him. The front man of the four, wearing a mismatched suit, was holding a machine gun loosely in one hand while passing Batista a bulging carry bag with the other.

'Our sources confirm what we already suspected, that Batista's working on expanding his operation, with the help of overseas funding. Being linked with the hijacking has raised his profile and he's come up as a blip on the radar.' Jack handed Ben a thick red folder with SPECIAL OPS EVENT 0309 in bold letters across the front cover, and indicated they take a seat.

Already scanning the folder's contents, Ben lowered himself into a chair at the U-shaped meeting table.

Sitting opposite him, Jack lowered his voice despite the room's soundproofing. 'The powers-that-be have issued a neutralisation order, following a number of failed attempts to apprehend Batista. They want him and his operation shut down before he gets too big and out of control. They're striving to eliminate all known threats prior to the G20 Summit, and in light of his involvement with the hijacking, they now believe

Batista is a credible threat and a potential embarrassment.'

Still gazing at the information in the folder, Ben nodded without speaking.

'He'll be back in Australia in four weeks' time, and will probably go straight to his country retreat in the Blue Mountains, outside of Katoomba. Our surveillance shows he's implemented some serious security measures on-site. There've been up to eight heavily-armed security guards spotted at different times, depending on who's in residence or visiting.' Sitting back, Jack eyed Ben intently. 'Beta team has been assigned the event. When Batista lands back here in Oz, you are to handle it in the usual manner. I'll keep you informed of any new intel that comes our way, but that file,' and he pointed to the folder in Ben's hand, 'contains everything we have on him at the moment.'

Flicking to the last page of the file, Ben glanced up with a frown. 'There's not much here.'

Jack shrugged a broad, suit-coated shoulder. 'He hasn't been big enough for us to bother with him much … until now.' He pointed at the folder. 'That intel has only been put together in the last month. You'll also find information on his overseas movements, along with some … disturbing … surveillance video on the network drive.'

Ben nodded and closed the folder with a snap.

'Understood. How soon after he lands do you want this actioned?'

'Within a month.'

The two men nodded and rose to their feet.

As they headed to the door Jack asked, 'How's the new recruit going? She looks physically tough, and strikes me as the resilient type.' His tone grew doubtful. 'Prettier than I expected, though.'

Ben gave a wry snort. 'Don't worry about JD. When it comes to a crisis situation, she's one of the most capable and level-headed soldiers I've worked with. If I had any doubts about her ability she wouldn't be here.' At Jack's brusque nod, Ben asked, 'Have you met Leroy, the martial arts instructor?'

'The big American Negro?'

Ben nodded.

'I've met him. An impressive-looking bloke.' Jack raised a roguish eyebrow. 'Ever thought about recruiting him?'

'He's a big guy, no denying.' Ben grinned. 'But our new recruit had him on his knees and tapping out within the first ten minutes of this morning's class.'

Jack stopped in the doorway and stared at Ben in amusement. 'Is that right?'

'Yep. Leroy was a bit red-faced telling me about it; reckons he's going to treat her with more respect from now on. I told him not to worry, he isn't the first one to underestimate her and he won't be the last.'

'Good for her.' Jack thumped Ben on the back. 'And point taken.'

They left together, and when they reached his office doorway Ben said, 'I'll monitor her progress over the next couple of weeks, but as far as an assignment like this is concerned,' and he held up the folder, 'our new recruit will have no problems tackling it right now. It should be an easy first mission for her.'

'That's your call,' Jack said crisply, 'this is your mission now.' He fixed Ben with a steely gaze. 'And I'm sure I don't need to tell you that this is a need-to-know operation. As usual, if anything goes wrong, the powers-that-be will deny any knowledge of it.'

'Understood.'

Seated at his desk, Ben opened the file again. Logging into his computer, he found the surveillance footage in the EVENT 0309 network folder and set the video to play. Most of the footage showed Batista entering seedy establishments accompanied by bearded, turban-clad guards armed with AK47s. Ben paused the video occasionally to check images against the file of Batista's known associates, and again when the clearest shot of Batista himself came into view. He leaned closer to the screen to stare at the image. Every inch of the thug's visible skin was covered in black hair or stubble. The chains around his neck appeared to be embedded in rolls of fat, and his open, large-lapelled shirt revealed a bloated, pock-marked belly. His bulbous, turned-up nose in the centre of a round, greasy face, along with his toothy sneer, did nothing to detract from his brutish appearance.

When he pressed PLAY, the video advanced, and Ben watched Batista's thick lips twist cruelly as he gave a harsh, grunting laugh.

Ben's own lip curled.

The guy even looks like a pig.

When that footage ended, Ben opened another video capture, listed as being 'From a makeshift firing range in Somalia'. In it, a supercilious-looking Batista stood in front of a group of turban-clad guerrillas holding an RPG-7 launcher. Throwing his audience a fiendish smirk, he turned and fired at the burnt-out wreck of what looked to be an early model Mercedes sedan. The rocket-propelled grenade exploded as it hit its mark, turning the car into a fiery ball of molten metal fragments.

The pointless destruction appeared to fill the guerrillas with primitive exhilaration. They went wild, dancing and waving their arms, chanting and firing their AK47s into the sky. Ben shook his head at the infantile behaviour, and then did a double-take. A figure in the distance had caught his eye. He rewound the video and zoomed in, but the resolution was poor and the image too grainy for proper identification. All the same, the dark figure, silhouetted against the sky as it strode away, brought on a strong sense of familiarity.

Ben re-ran the footage a few more times, before finally dismissing it and moving on.

The next file he opened, titled INTEL: SEIZED 2013, contained footage of a Sudanese girl of around ten years of age. Lying on a filthy mattress in a dimly-lit room, she was wailing and struggling against the over-weight and equally filthy man holding her down. His intentions toward her were obvious from his licentious expression and slack, slobbering mouth. When the camera panned to the right, it captured a clearly delighted Batista looking on from where he sat at the back of the room.

Repulsed, Ben averted his eyes and muttered through clenched teeth, 'Now I *really* hate the bastard.'

He switched off the footage and forced his mind to return to the mission. Pulling up an aerial photo of Batista's Blue Mountains property, he printed an A3-sized coloured copy. After laying it flat on his desk, he placed an open protractor against the scale in the photo's bottom corner. Turning back to the computer, he brought up the latest satellite image of Batista's hacienda-styled home and zoomed-in first to the roof top, and then to one of the guards stationed there. His eyes narrowed as he took in the guard's weapon.

M4 Carbine ... an effective range of approximately five hundred metres.

Using the protractor he drew a circle, scaled to seven hundred metres, around the hacienda, followed by another circle at nine hundred metres. Then he sat back to stare at the marked-up photo.

Isolated location ... that's good ... and scope to engage the enemy from almost any direction. Should be plenty of vantage points to take a shot and stay out of the effective range of standard small arms fire.

He tapped the protractor against the palm of his hand.

If I send in more than one operative, it's likely to turn into a bloodbath. This mission calls for a single decisive strike by one agent.

Sitting forward again, he rested his tanned arms on the desk.

By the time Batista's back in Australia, JD will've finished her induction. Teamed with her military experience, that makes this assignment right up her alley. It's what she's being trained for. So ... should I help her plan her strategy?

He rubbed his chin and stared at the photo.

She'll be the one on the ground doing the recon. That puts her in a much better position to make the call.

Decision made, he logged off the computer and slipped the A3 photo into the event file.

CHAPTER THIRTEEN

Modeen wandered into the staff kitchen and was about to grab a cup from the shelf when she glimpsed a big man march past. She called, 'Wolf!' and heard his footsteps halt.

Ambling back along the corridor, he leaned against the doorjamb and smiled lazily at her.

'So, how was the session with Pierre?'

Shaking his head at her impish grin, he growled, 'We both survived the encounter. What about you and whatshername?'

'Vivienne. Yeah, the same. We just finished our session.' Her left eyebrow twitched. 'So I take it there'll be no *cuisses de grenouille* on the menu tonight?' At his puzzled expression, she said, 'That's French for Frogs' Legs.'

'Oh.' He straightened and gave a roguish half smile. 'No, not tonight.' Stepping into the room, he headed to the table and pulled out a chair. Bowing, he indicated the chair with a sweep of his tattooed arm. 'Please take a seat *mademoiselle*. And would you allow me the pleasure of making you a coffee?'

Swallowing a grin, she dropped a curtsy and gushed, 'But of course, *mon cher.*' Placing one hand on her hip and raising the other with a dramatic sweep, she stuck her nose in the air and sashayed to the table with an exaggerated swing of slim hips.

They laughed together, until Wolf pushed in her chair and she found herself pinned between the backrest and the table. She looked up at him with a bemused expression and he hastily pulled her chair back, saying gruffly, 'Sorry. Need to work on my "finesse", or so LeMar tells me.'

Even hearing Wolf say the word 'finesse' was a new experience. Resting both hands demurely in her lap, she watched him take two steps back, bowing as he went. When he straightened and threw her a wink, she spluttered into laughter and he joined her.

With a droll, 'Very funny, you clowns,' Ben strode into the room, having watched their performance from the doorway. 'At least it looks like you're learning something.' This met with more laughter and he waited for it to subside. Throwing them a wry glance, he said, 'Keep practising, 'cos you'll be given an exercise to demonstrate your competence in civilian covert ops.'

Modeen's eyes lit up. 'Details?'

Moving to the counter, he proceeded to make himself a hot drink. 'All I can say at this stage is that you'll be posing as a married couple at a high-society, invitation-only social event.' Releasing the tap on the urn, he stirred his coffee and glanced over his shoulder at them. 'And it won't be all hors d'oeuvres, champers and hobnobbing. You'll be part of the ASIS security team.'

Modeen eyed him speculatively as he took a sip from his mug. 'ASIS? So there'll be some VIPs at this shindig?'

'I'll have more details for you when you get back from Swan Island.'

She nodded and then her expression lifted. Rolling her eyes, she moaned, 'Married to Wolf ... *great.*'

'You should be so lucky.' Wolf tried to look peeved but his twitching lips gave him away.

With an amused grunt, Ben drained his mug and rubbed his hands together. 'Right, I'm taking my old unit buddies out to lunch. Where would you like to go?'

'It's your turf, Corporal,' Wolf said amiably, 'lead the way.'

'Right-o. You up for a walk?' At their nods, Ben rinsed his mug in the sink and announced, 'Let's go then.'

• • •

As usual, Lygon Street, often referred to as Melbourne's Eat Street, bustled with diners strolling the footpaths and studying the carefully prepared menu boards, restaurateurs yelling inducements from their doorways, and delivery vans disgorging crates of fresh produce. The tantalising aromas of garlic, char-grilling meat, and wood-fired pizza hung in the air, working their magic on hungry passers-by.

As they sauntered past several aromatic cafés and restaurants, Ben said, 'Anyone who can't find tempting food on this street is impossible to please.'

From one doorway a short, chubby-cheeked man stepped onto the footpath in front of them, waving a bottle of wine. 'Free wine with-a your meal!' he called eagerly in a heavy Greek accent. 'Come, eat! Best food on Lygon Street.'

Ben didn't slow his pace, merely raising a hand and stepping around the little man, who continued yelling inducements at their backs. When they got to a softly-lit Italian café, Ben stopped and ushered them in, saying, 'Emily reckons the lasagne here is the best.'

Wolf smacked his lips. 'Sounds like a challenge. I'm up for it.'

As they were led to a window table looking out into the busy street, Ben bent his head to say quietly to the waitress, 'Any chance we could have that table in the back corner?'

The petite young woman blushed, clearly overawed by his height and commanding presence. Chirping, 'Of course sir,' she led them to the table he'd indicated, hastily removing a reserved sign and dropping it onto a nearby table.

Ben frowned. 'Sorry. I didn't realise this one was reserved.'

'They won't mind,' the waitress said brightly, batting her eyelashes at him.

'Well, thanks.' When he smiled down at her, she turned a deeper shade of pink, giggled, and skipped off to get them some menus.

Wolf dug him in the ribs. 'For an old married man, ya still got it, mate.'

Ben just gave a snort and shook his head.

As they sat back, finishing their complimentary bottle of Shiraz, Modeen said, 'Emily nailed it, I gotta say. That lasagne was divine,' and she held up her wine glass. 'Here's to Emily.'

They clinked glasses and Wolf drawled, 'Just look at us, will ya? Who would'a thought a bunch of green-grass Army recruits would end up here.'

'There's been a lot of water under the bridge since we were raw recruits.' Modeen shot Ben a glance. 'And life doesn't look to be getting boring any time soon.'

'Yep, there's always plenty to do.' Ben leaned forward and kept his voice low. 'Take the opportunities when you're not on assignment to hone your skills. Just let me know and I'll arrange refreshers or additional training for you, whether it's another high altitude jump, a stint on the range, SCUBA dive, or you want to get your pilot's licence – whatever. In order to succeed, we need to stay up-skilled as well as fit and sharp-witted.' He turned to Wolf. 'How do you feel about going back to Swan Island next week with JD? I've run it past your team leader, he's okay with it.'

Wolf shrugged a brawny shoulder. 'No problem. I don't mind doin' a refresher.' He glanced at Modeen. 'We'll get to play with some cool stuff. Last time I was there I learnt some new things, like knife throwin' techniques, and how to turn a kitchen microwave into a handy little bomb.'

'Sounds good.' She gave a slow, approving nod. 'How far is the island from here?'

'Only about an hour and a half's drive. It's just on the other side of Port Phillip Bay.' Wolf flicked Ben a suggestive glance. 'And has a nice golf course.' At Ben's raised eyebrow, he continued. 'I'm thinkin' that we might be able to get in a couple of rounds, if we have time?'

'By all means. You never know when being able to play golf – or any sport for that matter – might come in handy. But remember, it isn't an island holiday, you're there for training.' Ben leaned closer. 'Try to organise a night dive or two while you're there. It's possible some black water ops might come up in the near future.'

At their nods, he sat back and swallowed the last of his wine. Rolling the empty glass around in his hands, he mused, 'You know, it was on Swan Island that Gator honed his explosives skills.' Putting down the glass, he fixed Modeen with a level gaze. 'And speaking of Gator, I've had some disturbing news.'

Without realising she was doing it, she held her breath.

'Did you know he suffered from PTSD?'

She blinked and lowered her eyes. 'He never admitted it, but I had my suspicions.' She looked up at Ben again. 'On our last mission, he told me on the quiet that he was having trouble adjusting to home life, and felt he couldn't put a foot right with Denise. On his most recent leave, he'd taken her out for a date night, but then blew up at her in front of everyone in a busy restaurant when she complained about her meal being poorly presented – missing a garnish or some such thing. You know how picky she could be, being a trained pastry chef herself.'

The men nodded as Modeen went on. 'Anyway, Gator said after witnessing the effects of famine in third world countries, and seeing the maggot-ridden offerings some people are forced to eat, he lost it, right there in the restaurant. He couldn't believe his wife could reject a meal for such a trivial reason.'

Grim-faced, Ben shook his head. 'His mother told me Gator had taken to yelling at the kids for crying over petty things, and then he and Denise would end up in a shouting match. It got so that Denise didn't know what he was going to do next, and she couldn't cope. She hit the bottle pretty hard, which only made matters worse. After they separated, Gator stayed with his mother for a while before re-enlisting for another two years. Guess he went back to military life 'cos he felt he belonged there.'

All three sat in thoughtful silence, until Ben eventually spoke up. 'Post-traumatic stress disorder is a common psychiatric problem facing returned soldiers.' He fixed them with a stern glance. 'If you guys ever feel you need to talk, you contact me, don't hesitate. I won't think any less of you for it. We have some very good people on hand, who treat every case with the utmost confidentiality.' He paused when the waitress appeared and buzzed around them, collecting their empty plates. He caught her eye. It wasn't hard. 'Could we have some coffees?'

'Certainly, sir.' The young woman beamed at him as she reached into her pocket and pulled out a notepad. Taking a pen from behind her ear, she tore her eyes away from Ben to take their orders.

As she hurried back to the kitchen, Wolf leaned forward to say, 'Don't get me wrong. Gator was a bloody good digger and a great mate, but to me he always seemed to be a sort of … intellectual type, and a bit highly-strung for a soldier.' He glanced down at the table and said brusquely, 'Sure, I've had some restless nights since leaving the Force, but for the most part I can leave it all behind … what we did, what we saw.' He raised his eyes again. 'Guess I'm lucky like that, and Gator not so. How about you, Modeen?'

'When I'm in civvies,' she said slowly, 'I'm comfortable with who I am. In uniform, my whole focus is on the job I'm expected to do, and on being an effective squad member. When I lost friends or witnessed atrocities, I told myself we were serving the greater good … that we were fighting for freedom, and the protection of our friends and families back home.'

'Well said, JD.' Ben put a hand on her shoulder. 'And you'll be doing the same now, only the enemy is closer to home and not usually in uniform.'

The waitress, now wearing freshly applied pink lipstick, arrived to serve their hot drinks. First she placed a cappuccino with a crema-coloured heart design in the froth, in front of Ben. Then she served the other two their coffees, both sporting leaf patterns.

With an amused roll of eyes, Wolf grasped his cup in a large hand, making it look like it came from a child's tea set. Taking a mouthful, he savoured it and remarked, 'This is a far cry from the crap the ration assassins served up in the Army.'

Ben nodded and set down his mug. 'So,' he said mildly, 'what's on for you guys this afternoon?'

'James is going to take us over some spy gadgets and software.' Modeen licked froth from her top lip. 'Our schedule is basically the same for the rest of the week. Leroy in the mornings, followed by our lessons with LeMar and Vivienne, then finish the afternoons with James.' She threw Ben a self-conscious grin. 'Which of course you already knew.' Receiving a smile in reply, she turned to Wolf. 'Say … talking about schedules. Are you staying at Rydges?'

'Yep, room six-o-five.'

'I'm in six-ten. You up for a morning run, say o-six hundred?'

'Sure. I'll meet ya in the lobby.'

CHAPTER FOURTEEN

'Greetings, students.' In the centre of the mat, Leroy pressed his hands together and bowed over them. 'As this is our last day, we will be putting into practice the skills we have learned over the week.' He inclined his head toward the woman standing silent and expressionless at his side, her white judogi cinched at the waist with a black fabric belt. 'We have Kimiko Ishikawa joining us today. Kimiko is a sixth dan black belt and an expert in Karate and Ju-Jitsu.'

After another group bow, Leroy announced, 'This mornin' we will start with our usual warm-up and then have a light sparring session.'

Modeen watched Kimiko during the warm-up. Tall for a Japanese woman, she moved with a lithe, restrained grace that hinted at ability.

A short time later Leroy resumed his place in the centre of the mat and clapped his hands. 'Now for the sparring session.' He gazed into each of the expectant faces around him. 'Use what you've learned against your opponent if you can, but remember,' and he raised a cautionary finger, 'we're all friends here, so take care to pull your punches and your kicks. I don't want anyone carted off in an ambulance today. Are we clear on that?' At their nods, he barked, 'Right,' and gestured to Modeen. 'Ladies first.'

Rising, she positioned herself at the opposite side of the mat from Kimiko and the two women locked gazes, sizing each other up. They were well matched in height, with Modeen only marginally taller than the sinewy, poker-faced Kimiko. When Leroy moved to stand between them and instructed them to bow, they obeyed, keeping their eyes fixed on each other.

Watching from the edge of the mat, Wolf leaned toward Craig seated nearby and murmured, 'This ought'a be good.'

Putting his hand in the air between the two contestants, Leroy shouted *'Hajime!'* and then jogged backward to give them space.

The two contestants maintained eye contact as they circled the mat, staying an even distance from each other. Kimiko made the first move. Taking a step back, she took a boxer-like karate stance, arms raised and fists clenched, and then came at her opponent.

As she sprang into the air and unleashed a lighting-fast side kick, Modeen stepped back and tapped Kimiko's foot down with her hand, as though swatting a fly. The black belt immediately followed up with a round-house kick to the temple, which Modeen intercepted with a double arm block. Instantly Kimiko aimed another round-house kick at her stomach. When Modeen lifted her knee and blocked the strike, an audible crack resonated from the sharp contact, making the spectators wince.

After limping back two steps, shaking her foot, Kimiko darted in with straight-arm jabs at her opponent's head. Modeen ducked sideways for the first blow and intercepted the second with an arm-lock. When Kimiko let out a yelp, Modeen released her, only to be tricked into a reverse arm bar. As Kimiko applied more pressure to the hold, Modeen grimaced and bent forward at the waist. This put her face close to Wolf's at the edge of the mat.

Leaning forward, he said in her ear, 'What the hell you doin'? You're better than this.'

Still grimacing, she puffed, 'I've never fought a woman before.'

Throwing Kimiko a menacing glance he growled, 'Just think of her as a man ... and kick his *ass!*'

She was frowning dubiously at Wolf when she felt Kimiko increase the pressure on her arm. Swung forward into the centre of the mat, she kept the momentum going and propped to launch herself into a forward somersault, reversing Kimiko's grip on her arm mid-air. Landing squarely in a crouched position in front of her opponent, she brought her left arm down and backward, pulling Kimiko toward her as she thrust upward and forward. She rolled her shoulders, executing a perfect *Ippon Seoi Nage,* and Kimiko landed flat on her back with a wince-inducing crunch and a grunt as the air was punched from her lungs.

Maintaining her hold on Kimiko's arm, Modeen clasped her hand in a wrist lock. This time when the black belt let out a yelp, Modeen increased the pressure until Kimiko tapped the side of her leg. Releasing her hold, Modeen stepped back to her side of the mat and watched as Kimiko rose unsteadily to her feet.

Leroy nodded his head at Modeen, exclaiming, 'Very good! You have a natural ability and smoothness about your style.'

The two women shared a bow and then Modeen resumed her seat beside Wolf, as Leroy gestured to him.

'Care to join me on the mat, Troy?'

Uncurling from his seated position with a grace uncommon for a man his size, Wolf positioned himself facing Leroy. Kimiko came to stand between them, tugging her judogi to straighten it and pointedly ignoring Modeen.

The two men bowed to each other as Kimiko raised her arm and held it at a right angle to her body. Eyeing them intently, she dropped her arm, commanded, *'Hajimi!'* and took two quick steps backward.

Leroy bounced on his toes on the spot, keeping his legs straight and shaking his hands loosely by his sides in a confident warm-up gesture. He rolled his shoulders and then his head from left to right to loosen his neck muscles, all the while staying attuned to the movements of his thirty pounds lighter and two inches shorter opponent.

Modeen watched them size each other up.

This should be interesting.

An instant later, Leroy dropped his casual air and went on the attack. Turning side-on, he shuffled toward Wolf, who stepped back and sideways to match him. Leaping forward, Leroy landed a metre from Wolf and aimed a high-speed side kick at his head.

Flicking his head to the right, Wolf blocked the strike with his open hand and caught hold of Leroy's leg, locking it at shoulder height and putting his opponent off-balance. Stepping forward, he delivered a powerful palm thrust to the big man's chest while simultaneously sweeping his other leg out from under him, sending him crashing to the floor.

Wolf moved into the centre of the mat, keeping his eyes glued on the winded Leroy, who sat up and coughed and then rose, shaking his head. Once upright, he took his time bowing and assuming a defensive Karate stance.

Standing with bent knees in the centre of the mat, his eyes dark slits as he stared at his opponent, Wolf readied himself as Leroy moved in, displaying less bravado and more caution this time. As before, Wolf turned side-on, to give himself a balanced stance and provide his challenger with a smaller target. Leroy moved closer, waiting for the right moment, and then lunged forward, aiming three kicks at Wolf's ribs.

With each one, Wolf stepped backward in perfect synchronisation, swatting the kicks with the palms of his hands.

Right.

Left.

Right again.

Then, after the final kick, Wolf sprang sideways. When the advancing Leroy pivoted to follow him, Wolf lunged forward and rammed his elbow against Leroy's shoulder, sending him staggering sideways. Without taking his eyes off the instructor, Wolf moved backward to the edge of the mat and jogged on the spot, giving Leroy time to regain his composure.

Shaking his head, Leroy tugged his black judo suit straight and turned to face Wolf. 'Very good.' He nodded. 'You have fast reflexes.' He took up position and barked, 'Again.'

This time, he took a more judo-like approach. Once within reach, he snaked out an arm and caught hold of Wolf's lapel. When Wolf tried to brush off the hold, Leroy intercepted the move and pulled him in close. Rolling his shoulders and then his body as he dropped to his knees, Leroy made to throw his opponent over his shoulder. Instantly Wolf dropped his weight in behind Leroy, and they were at a stalemate.

Taking advantage of the moment, Wolf glanced

over at Modeen and found her watching intently. He threw her a wink and moved his weight higher.

She frowned at him, puzzled.

Why was he purposefully giving Leroy the advantage?

Sliding over Leroy's shoulders, Wolf pulled him down to the mat and they rolled together, each struggling to gain the upper hand. When Wolf attempted an arm-bar hold, Leroy scissored him between his legs, trapped his arm, and proceeded to lock him in a strangle hold. He then pulled down on Wolf's arm and arched his back, making Wolf grimace and tap the side of his leg. Leroy immediately released his grip and they disentangled themselves.

After they resumed their respective positions and shared a bow, Leroy announced, 'That manoeuvre was *Sankaku Jime,* the triangular strangle.' Then he turned to Craig and Wyatt and beckoned them to face each other on the mat.

As Wolf took his seat next to Modeen, she nudged his shoulder with hers and said quietly, 'You're just a big old softy, letting him get one over you like that.'

He gave a wry grunt and then murmured, 'Guys like Leroy tend to get lots of practice but not much real fighting experience. And when they over-estimate their abilities they get into all sorts of trouble.' He crinkled his chin thoughtfully. 'Leroy seems genuine enough, though.' Turning to Modeen, he raised an insouciant eyebrow. 'At least *I* didn't humiliate him on our first day.'

She arched an eyebrow at him and said nothing.

'Well … that's our martial arts training down.' Wolf leaned back against the kitchen counter and raised his cup to his lips.

'Yep.' Modeen eyed him. 'Hey, has Ben given you any more details about the soiree we're supposed to attend?'

'Only that it's being held in Brisbane the week after we get back from Swan Island.'

She nodded.

After swallowing a mouthful of coffee he mused aloud, 'I wonder what sort of torture LeMar and Vivienne have planned for us today.'

'We'll find out soon enough.'

'D'you know why they want us both in the same trainin' room this time?'

She frowned. 'In the same room? All four of us?'

'That's what Ben said. Just didn't say why.'

The crease in Modeen's brow deepened, and then she breathed out in a resigned whoosh. 'Oh, great.'

'What?'

'Our upcoming mission's not just at any old function, it's at a *high society* function.'

'Yeah, so?'

'Where there's bound to be *dancing?*' When his

perplexed expression didn't change, she shook her head and sighed. 'What's the bet we're in for dance lessons.' She looked at him doubtfully. 'You ever done any dancing, of the ballroom variety?'

'As a matter of fact, I have.' Straightening, he flicked her a narrow-eyed glance. 'Don't look so surprised. Mum insisted on me and my brother takin' dance classes when we were kids ... for a much-needed dose of culture, she said. Turned out I had some aptitude. Not that I tell many people that.'

'*You*, Troy Wolverton, a ballroom dancer?'

At her stifled laughter, he glowered down his nose at her. 'Why's that so funny?'

'Sorry,' she spluttered, 'but having met you in the Army, I just ... never imagined you as a twinkle-toes.'

'Is that so?' Swallowing a grin, he puffed out his chest and crossed his brawny arms over it. 'Well, the curtain's about to be lifted.'

She gave a belly laugh. 'This'll be something to see.'

His derisive, 'Humph,' was spoiled by the lopsided grin he could no longer contain. Uncrossing his arms, he leaned back against the counter again. 'Now, what are you doin' over the weekend? Headin' back home to the Gold Coast?'

Still grinning, she took a sip of coffee before saying thoughtfully, 'While I'm here I might check out some more of the sights around Melbourne. I've heard Mount Buffalo is worth seeing, with views of the Australian Alps from the top. And the town of Bright is meant to be pretty at this time of year.' She glanced at him over the rim of her cup. 'What about you?'

'Flyin' to Hobart. Harper's droppin' me at the airport straight after this session. I'll be back Sunday night.'

Modeen nodded. 'What say we meet here Monday morning, o-six hundred. We'll take my car to Swan Island.'

With a gruff, 'Sounds good to me,' Wolf drained his cup, as a fashionably dressed man with slicked-back hair sauntered past, conversing in fluent French with the high-heeled fashionista at his side.

CHAPTER FIFTEEN

When she saw Wolf enter via the stairwell, Modeen finished giving her Aurion the once-over and leaned both arms on the car's roof. As he came striding, long-legged, across the NatSec carpark, she glanced at her watch.

O-five forty-nine.

Prompt, as always.

He stopped to let another vehicle pass and threw her a resigned look. There was always more activity at HQ on Monday mornings, with agents reporting in for the week.

When he jogged over to join her at the Aurion, she greeted him with a lift of her chin and received a gruff, 'Hey,' and dip of his dark head in reply.

'How was the trip to Hobart?'

Grumbling, 'Families,' he rolled his eyes. 'I'll tell you about it after we hit the road.'

She tapped the roof with both hands. 'Right then, let's go.' Jumping into the driver's seat, she started the car and reversed smoothly out of the parking bay. They glided up the exit ramp, and while waiting for the roller door to open, she swept a glance over his large, familiar form in the passenger seat beside her. Turning back to watch the door rise, she murmured, 'When we get there, we're supposed to meet with Secret Service representative Ross Wentworth.'

Wolf gave a grunt. 'Yeah, met 'im last time. He and his crew seemed like an okay bunch, but some of that interrogation training they put me through got a bit nasty.' He flicked her a glance.

'Interrogation? You mean we're gonna be trained in that as well?'

As she accelerated out onto the street, he gave a throaty chuckle. 'Yep, trained how to interrogate others, and how to handle bein' interrogated ourselves. There are some interestin' techniques for blockin' out pain....' Gazing through the window at the dark, barely stirring city, he added, 'Last time I was there, it got pretty intense. They had me tied to a chair with a canvas bag over my head, then they doused me with water ... and doused me again ... and again. Surprisin' what effect almost drownin' has on ya.' At her sideways frown, he shrugged one beefy shoulder. 'It's just good trainin'. Drives home the situations we might find ourselves in, which is the message they want to get across, I guess.'

She chewed her bottom lip. 'All the same, I'm not looking forward to that.'

He glanced over at her and then back out the window. 'Nothin' you can't handle. Just keep your cool and you'll be alright. Anyway, the interrogation stuff's only a small part of what we'll be doin'.'

She nodded. 'I haven't been to Swan Island base before. What's it like?'

'Fairly nondescript, includin' the buildings ... what you can see of them, that is. Doesn't look like much on the surface, but the base is one of Australia's most secret facilities, shared by the Secret Intelligence Service and Special Forces. There's a huge subterranean network underground, connected by a labyrinth of tunnels.'

Modeen kept her eyes on the road. 'So ... where does NatSec fit in?'

Wolf pondered the question before replying, 'It's somehow affiliated with ASIS and ASIO, but how that affiliation is structured is anybody's guess. Given the work we do, I can understand why they don't want anyone to know who's pullin' the strings.'

'Makes sense.' They travelled in silence for a while and then she prompted, 'So, what's up with your brother in Tassie?'

Wolf sighed. 'Look, I know they've got their own lives to live and their own priorities, but how can two brothers from the same parents grow up to be so different.' Scowling, he stared unseeingly out the window.

'Jake and his wife have a little mutt of a dog they treat better than people. It shits inside the house and drags its ass along the carpet.'

Turning to see Modeen bite back laughter, he raised an eyebrow at her and growled, 'Yeah, funny right? Unless you're expected to lay your swag on the same carpet.' He gave a disparaging snort. 'Jake whinges about the mongrel but doesn't bother to train it, just lets it rule the household. I think he's afraid of upsettin' his wife. She's obsessed with the mutt, buys it sparkly collars 'n crap like that.' He gave a slow, disapproving shake of his head. 'Jake never used to be such a wuss.' He fixed Modeen with an intense gaze. 'Get this, I'm sittin' at the table and the overfed little mongrel growls at me, then nips me on the ankle when I won't give it any of the food off my plate.'

'What did you do?'

Wolf's eyes gleamed wickedly as he said with exaggerated innocence, 'Merely suggested a quick fix for my brother's problem.' With a thumb and two fingers he made the shape of a gun and acted out taking a shot.

She flicked him a wide-eyed glance. 'Oh-oh.'

'Yeah.' He shrugged. 'They went ballistic when all I was doin' was showin' them how easy it would be to dispatch the useless little shit.' He gave a disgruntled sniff while struggling to keep a roguish grin in check. 'Apparently I'm not welcome back there any time soon.' Lifting one dark, sardonic brow, he added, 'And that's fine by me.'

On reaching Geelong, they stopped for breakfast before heading down the Bellarine highway toward Queenscliffe. When they reached the first checkpoint on Main Road, just before the bridge connecting the mainland to Rabbit and Swan islands, they joined a queue of cars stopped at a partial boom gate. A uniformed attendant was talking to the driver of the first vehicle, a BMW sedan.

Wolf muttered, 'Security's pretty low at this first checkpoint. Most people comin' across are either going to Queenscliffe golf club or to the wharf on the other side of the harbour.'

Modeen wound down her window and heard the attendant say, 'You're a member sir?' Nodding at the response, the attendant made a note on his clipboard. 'Straight ahead and to the left, sir.' When he nodded at a second attendant in the security booth, the boom lifted. Waving the car through, the attendant approached the next vehicle in the queue as the boom dropped behind him.

Leaning in to speak to the driver of the dual cab four wheel drive, the attendant asked, 'Purpose of visit, sir?' After pausing to listen he wrote on his clipboard again. 'Name?'

Another notation.

'And you're the owner of the boat?'

Another scribble and a nod to the second attendant. 'Straight ahead and then a U-turn to the right, sir.' With that he waved the four wheel drive on.

As Modeen nosed the Aurion forward, the attendant leaned in the driver's window to look at them both. 'Purpose of visit Ma'am?'

'We have an appointment at the Swan Island facility.'

The man turned over a page on his clipboard. 'Names?'

'Josephine Bennet and Troy Ryan.'

'And your contact on the base?'

'Ross Wentworth.'

After jotting something down, the attendant straightened and nodded toward the booth. 'Straight ahead, Ma'am, and then to the second checkpoint on the right.' With his attention already focused on the vehicle behind them, he waved them through the rising boom gate.

They crossed the first bridge to Rabbit Island, the smaller of the two, and then the second to Swan Island.

At Wolf's, 'Feel like I'm back in the Florida Keys,' Modeen murmured, 'Reminds me of Naval Fleet Base West, on Garden Island in WA.'

A large signpost at the Swan Island end of the bridge showed the way to the golf club, harbour, and military base. In the distance they saw the BMW cruising toward the golf club, while immediately ahead of them the four wheel drive made a sharp U-turn onto the harbour road.

They turned right toward the base and were immediately confronted by another red and white striped boom gate. Unlike the first boom, this one covered the whole width of the road, while the gatehouse beside it sported a plethora of warning notices.

As the Aurion slowed to a stop, the armed guard standing in front of the boom came forward, scrutinising the car as he approached. Keeping his rifle shouldered, the soldier leaned in to eyeball the vehicle's passengers.

'You NatSec?'

He'd obviously recognised the car.

Modeen nodded. In reply to his rapped, 'IDs and purpose of visit,' she passed him their NatSec IDs and said pleasantly, 'Josephine Bennet and Troy Ryan, to meet with Ross Wentworth.'

After checking their faces against their photos, the guard said, 'Wait here, Ma'am.' He disappeared into the guard house and she saw him speaking on the phone. Moments later he returned and handed back their IDs. When the boom lifted he waved them through.

Modeen glanced at Wolf as she accelerated through the gate. 'What happens if someone tries to land here by boat?'

He gave a grunt. 'They'd be intercepted by the armed water patrol before they got anywhere near the island.' Flicking her a wicked grin, he added, 'And if they did somehow manage it, they'd give us subjects to practice our interrogation skills on.' At her incredulous look, he said, 'Well, the island *is* a training ground for counter-insurgency and guerrilla warfare, and I'm sure they like comin' up with new ways to scare the crap out of anyone stupid enough to try to infiltrate it.'

When they reached the main facility he pointed to a bay in the carpark. 'Pull in here. This is the admin block. We report here whenever we visit the base. Oh, and we have to leave our weapons, phones, cameras and any other recording devices in the car.'

They dropped their smart phones into the console as Modeen nosed the Aurion into the parking bay.

Wolf got out of the car and stretched. 'Wentworth shouldn't be too far away,' he drawled. 'He'll know we're here by now.'

They strolled into the reception area, which consisted of a small entry foyer, counter, and two visitor's chairs. The coffee table in front of the chairs was stacked with an assortment of military recruitment brochures.

Wolf picked one up and nudged Modeen. 'Challenge yourself,' he read aloud. 'Find the job that's right for you, in the Australian Army.' Tossing the brochure back onto the table, he muttered, 'Been there, done that, movin' on.'

At the counter to their left, a female soldier finished

subjecting them to an eagle-eyed perusal and said pleasantly, 'Good morning.'

Modeen approached the counter and dipped her head in greeting. 'Josephine Bennet and Troy Ryan, to meet with Ross Wentworth.'

The guard glanced at her computer screen. 'You're undertaking training on site this week, is that correct?' At Modeen's nod, the woman gestured to a monitor on her right displaying the white outline of a hand. 'Please identify yourselves.' After Modeen placed her hand on the scanner, the guard said, 'Thank you,' and looked at Wolf. As he stepped forward to do the same, the woman instructed, 'If you have any cameras, phones or recording devices, please leave them with me now.'

Seeing them shake their heads, the guard said crisply, 'So you don't have any of these items on your persons?' and they shook their heads again. 'Then please place all your metallic objects onto the conveyor near the revolving door,' and she pointed toward it. 'When you're ready, you can proceed through the door into the waiting room. You will be collected from there.'

Taking a plastic tray from the pile, they tossed their watches, wallets and keys into it and dropped it onto the conveyor belt, which rumbled into life. The revolving door turned slowly, allowing time for them to be scanned once more as they went through. On the other side, another guard stationed in the waiting room stood holding the tray. As he handed it to them he said, 'Please take a seat. You will be collected shortly.'

Almost straightaway a tall, well-built man entered the room through another revolving door. While sporting a military-style buzz-cut, he was dressed in civvies. Extending a suit-coated arm he said amiably, 'G'day Ryan. How long's it been?'

Wolf nodded, 'Wentworth,' and shook his hand. 'About eight months I'd reckon.' He inclined his head toward Modeen. 'This is Jo Bennet.'

'Good to meet you, Bennet.' Wentworth met and held her gaze as he shook her hand. 'Ben told me about your military achievements.' He nodded. 'Impressive.'

'Thanks, but I've been out for a while now. Hope I can live up to expectations.'

'I think you already have.' He dipped his head at her and then glanced at Wolf. 'Ben holds both of you in high regard, and we all know he's not easily impressed. Now, let's get going. Follow me.' Leading them to the revolving door he had entered through, he announced, 'And you guessed it, yet another scan.'

After entering the revolving door, he placed his hand on a screen in a recessed panel. There was a low buzz as the door rotated, allowing him through to the other side. Modeen waited until the door stopped before stepping into it. When she too placed her hand on it, the screen displayed a thumbnail of her passport photo in its top right corner. The door then buzzed and rotated, letting her through.

As Wolf followed suit, Wentworth called, 'This way,' and led them down a corridor and into a small room. A utilitarian metal desk covered in charts, paperwork, and a partially buried laptop sat beneath the room's only heavily barred window. After hastily clearing two chairs of bulging folders, which he promptly dumped on the floor in a corner, Wentworth muttered, 'This mess is my office. Have a seat,' as he dug under the paperwork.

Handing an itinerary and a crumpled map of the complex to Modeen, he then opened a drawer and took out two visitor passes on khaki-coloured lanyards. 'Keep these on you at all times while on base.' Passing them over, he rose to his feet. 'Troy's been through this already, but as this is your first time here, Jo, we'll do a quick tour before I take you to the explosives lab.' He strode out, saying over his shoulder, 'I've arranged a day dive for you on Tuesday, and a night dive with our dive team on Wednesday, so wear something appropriate … maybe bring a change of clothes with you. We have shower facilities on site you can use.'

He glanced back at them. 'You'll find we're pretty flexible about most things, so if there's anything you want to do that's not already on your itinerary, just let me know and I'll try to accommodate you. Any questions?'

Modeen looked at Wolf and then back at Wentworth. 'Do we have to go through all that sign-in palaver every day?'

'Yep, only you won't need me tagging along now you've got those visitor passes. And you'll find some of the buildings require more scans than others.' Stopping abruptly, he fixed them with a level gaze. 'Security is one thing we're *not* flexible about.'

As he turned and resumed walking, Modeen nudged Wolf and murmured, 'More scans … *great.*'

After a brief tour, Wentworth led them down two flights of stairs to a long, narrow concrete corridor. Starkly lit by florescent lights it connected to a small hub with two doors, one marked WEAPONS LAB and the other one, EXPLOSIVES.

CHAPTER SIXTEEN

At the sound of a door opening in the side of the admin building, Modeen and Wolf straightened from where they'd been leaning against the Aurion, and watched a man in camouflage fatigues bound down the stairs to make his way toward them with an air of suppressed energy. He wore his sleeves rolled up to darkly tanned elbows, and when he extended a hand to her, Modeen spotted the white Australian flag insignia of the RAN on his upper right sleeve.

'Paul Edwards. Navy clearance diver, and your guide for the day.'

'Jo Bennet, and this is Troy Ryan.'

'Bennet and Ryan, good to meet you.' After also shaking Wolf's large paw, Edwards said cheerfully, 'Ross asked me to take you guys on a dive this morning.' He slapped and then rubbed his hands together. 'And I've got something lined up that's a bit different from your average run-of-the-mill dive, that I think you'll find interesting.' He twitched an eyebrow at them. 'So if you'd like to pile into the wagon,' and he pointed to a Mercedes Benz G-wagon in camouflage colours parked a few bays up from their Aurion. 'I'll take you over to the dive facility.'

After speeding along the road to the northern-most point of the island, he slid the four wheel drive to a stop in front of a small concrete bunker about three hundred metres from the shoreline. Springing out, he checked they were following as he made for the bunker's massive steel security door. A muffled buzz came from within as he pressed a button to the right of the door, and a green LED illuminated on the camera mounted above the doorway. He stood shuffling his feet, waiting for a loud metallic grinding sound to cease, before tugging the two-inch thick door open and indicating for them to enter.

Once inside, they descended three flights of stairs to where the concrete 'tomb' opened into a huge underground cavern. Modeen and Wolf stopped and stared at the hundred metre-long, thirty metre-wide oceanic pool in the middle of the cavern.

Seeing Wolf nudge Modeen and indicate two racy-looking submersibles berthed on each side of the pool, Edwards said proudly, 'They're our seal carriers. Powered by three hundred and fifty horsepower diesel motors and Rolls Royce water jets. They'll do four knots under water, and over thirty on the surface.'

Wolf gave a low whistle and breathed, 'Cool ride.'

'That they are.' Edwards slapped him on the back. 'But sorry mate, we're not going out in them today. These are our ride.' He pointed to three torpedos mounted on ramps on top of a two metre-high platform.

'Bullshit!' Wolf turned incredulous eyes on him. *'Torpedos?* You're kiddin', aren't ya?'

Edwards' grin widened as he led them to the platform. 'These are NATO five thirty-three millimetre torpedo seals. Normally we'd stick you inside and shoot you out of a sub's torpedo tube, but today we're gonna launch straight from the ramps.'

As they climbed the stairs onto the platform they could see the ramps descending into the clear water of a second, shorter and narrower pool.

Edwards squatted beside the nearest torpedo and pointed at the controls inside it. 'The seals are simple to operate. Basically like riding a motorbike, only you're on your belly and there's no changing gears. They're equipped with GPS and depth gauges so you can't go wrong, even at night. The GPS gives a digital representation of your surroundings and will put you within half a metre of your target every time.' He sat back, slapped the side of the torpedo and turned to them with a smile. 'These babies have a range of ten nautical miles, but we'll only be doing six today.'

At their nods, he went on. 'Tomorrow you'll get to experience them on a night dive. For now, you'll find some tactical dry suits in the change rooms in there,' and he inclined his head toward a side door marked EQUIPMENT STORE. 'I'll get your rebreathers, masks and fins together. Once you're suited up, we'll meet back here for an induction and a dive brief.'

Modeen climbed the stairs, moving stiffly in her dry suit but knowing she'd soon be glad of its warm, dry protection. At the top of the platform, Edwards and Wolf stood waiting for her. The three of them donned their full-face masks and equipment, and then squeezed, feet-first and face-down, into their torpedo seals. Once snug inside his, Edwards switched on the comms headset built into his mask.

'Comms check, this is Edwards.'

'Comms check, Bennet.'

'Comms check, Ryan.'

Then another voice filled their earpieces. 'Launch team on standby, tube grate open, deploy on your command, sir.'

Modeen lifted her head and saw one of the launch team members standing expectantly nearby.

'Roger, just doing final checks.' Edwards glanced over at the other two pods. 'Bennet and Ryan, the coordinates have been logged into your GPS. We'll be doing a dogleg out to the first buoy, then across to the wreck and back. Just remember, maximum depth in these babies is eight metres. Once you're in the water, deploy your cockpit shield and guidance paddles. Oh, and don't forget to keep your heads down until we're in the water. Are we ready?'

'Bennet, ready.'

'Ryan ready.'

'Edwards ready. Launch team, we are go for launch.'

'Roger. Launching in five … four … three … two … one.' The crewman at the controls pressed the launch buttons, and the three in the pods lowered their heads as their seals began the downward slide.

Modeen felt the sudden rush as her torpedo gained speed and plunged into the pool, its momentum shooting it five metres through the water. As the bubbles subsided around her, Edwards' voice came over her headset.

'The exit tube is at the end of the pool. The grate in it will be open, and we'll go through single file. You might want to turn on your front light.' As the lights on all three torpedos blazed on, Edwards announced, 'I'll lead the way and wait for you on the other side.'

They followed him through the pool and into the mouth of a two-metre wide concrete stormwater pipe, emerging a hundred metres later into the deeper, cooler waters of the bay.

As they rendezvoused just outside the mouth of the pipe, Edwards said crisply, 'Depth three metres and viz fairly clear, around four metres.' He glanced at

Modeen's pod as it drew beside his. 'You getting the hang of it?'

'Yeah.' She lifted her head and gave him a thumbs-up. 'This is great.'

As Wolf pulled alongside them, muttering, 'These things aren't exactly lightning fast,' a defensive note crept into Edwards' voice.

'Their electric motors are powered by lithium polymer batteries, and considering their weight, four knots isn't bad. The seals will carry you ten nautical miles a lot faster than you can swim it. Of course we have more powerful submersibles that are a lot quicker, but they don't offer the convenience of being launched from a sub's torpedo tube.'

'Duly noted.'

'Right, let's go.' They cruised in arrowhead forma-tion, with Edwards in the lead and the other two on either side and a few metres behind him. When they reached the first buoy, they changed course and Edwards glanced back to make sure they were on track. 'If you want to take a closer look at the wreck, we can park the torpedos when we get there.'

'Sounds good.'

'Yeah.'

'Just remember to take your GPS units when you exit your seals, in case we forget where we parked,' he added wryly. 'Push the button on top of the unit and it'll pop forward out of its cradle. Just make sure not to lose—'

'WHAT THE—?' At Wolf's startled shout, Modeen's pulse quickened. She whipped her head around to see him peering through the water in all directions.

She barked into the comms, 'What's up?'

'Not sure, but … I might've just been dive-bombed by a shark.'

Edwards' calm voice came through their headsets. 'It's more than likely Freddy, our resident fur seal. He likes to check out newbies.'

'More like scare the crap out of 'em,' Wolf growled. 'Are you sure it was a seal? This thing was *really* movin'. All I saw was a flash of grey above my head, so close it nearly knocked my mask off.'

'Ahh … guys?' A tentative voice came over the comms. 'Is this … him?'

The men glanced over at Modeen. She was eye-to-eye with the fur seal floating effortlessly above her pod.

'Yep, that's Freddy.' Edwards grinned. 'Don't worry, he's friendly. This is why I thought it'd be a good idea to do a day dive first. Can you imagine what it's like being swooped by him during a pitch black night dive? He can still scare the crap outta me, and I'm usually expecting it.'

'What a lovely face, and such big brown eyes.' When Modeen reached a slow, tentative hand toward him, the seal let her put a fingertip to his fur before darting away again, leaving a trail of bubbles in his wake.

'Wow, you're privileged,' Edwards murmured. 'Fred doesn't normally let anyone get that close, especially if there aren't any tasty offerings to entice him.'

A short time later he announced over the comms, 'In the sand ahead you'll see the wreck of the Mountain Maid, lying where she fell.'

'What happened to her?' Modeen enquired.

'She was rammed by a steam ship.'

Wolf said drily, 'That'll do it.'

Landing their seals on the ocean floor they slid out, after first removing their GPS units and marking the location. As they swam to the wreck, Modeen noticed how few bubbles their rebreather units released. They also made very little sound.

Underwater stealth.

She spoke into her headset. 'Hey Edwards, how long are these rebreathers good for?'

'Depending on the diver, about an hour and a half at this depth.'

'Not much left of her, is there.' Wolf was ahead of them, already eyeing the wreck.

'No, not much at all. She's being entombed by the ocean. That's why they erected this in her honour, so she won't be forgotten.' Edwards indicated a stone plaque buried in the sea bed beside the ship's crustacean-covered remains. Thick, bold white letters were engraved on the black marble background. 'She was quite a handsome ship,' he mused aloud, 'it was a shame she went down. Apparently her captain was blamed for her demise and stripped of his commission.'

The three divers separated to inspect the Mountain Maid's scattered remains.

Minutes later Modeen called, 'Hey guys, check this out.' She was gazing over the edge of a nearby lime-stone shelf, at the sandy bottom three metres below.

At Wolf's gruff, 'What're we supposed to be lookin' at?' she pointed to a spot on the ocean floor. 'Stingray. Its outline is just visible, buried in the sand.'

He followed the direction of her finger and shrugged. 'Where?'

'There.'

'Think your seein' things.'

Edwards chimed in, 'I can't see anything either.'

'Oh, for— It's right *there.*' Modeen jabbed her finger in the same direction again, only to have Wolf shake his head and Edwards raise his hands in defeat.

Rolling her eyes, she snapped, 'I'll show you. Wait here, and *watch,*' as she slid over the edge of the shelf. She was within a metre of the sandy bottom when the whole sea floor came alive, making her jerk to a stop mid-water. From under the sand, a fever of more than a dozen stingrays flicked their muscular wings and took flight from their camouflaged slumber. Sand slid from their backs as they powered away from the intruder, creating a thick cloud of rising silt in their wake.

In her headpiece, Modeen heard muffled laughter and then Wolf spluttered, 'Oh right, *that* stingray.'

'Nice going, Bennet,' Edwards added, 'quite a performance,' and raised his gloved hands in applause while she glowered at them.

On their return to base some time later, their GPS units led them straight to the entrance pipe, where they once more flicked on their headlights and entered the tube in single file. As they emerged into the narrow oceanic pool inside the bunker, the security grate lowered behind them and, with a loud clank, locked off the tube entrance.

Modeen and Wolf powered down their pods to idle as Edwards put his into a sharp spin. They watched him reverse it onto the flat part of the conveyor on the launching ramp at the bottom of the pool, and took turns copying the manoeuvre. After sliding out of their seals, they swam over to join Edwards at the ladder. Grasping the handrail, they removed their fins before climbing the ladder and perching on the pool's edge. There, they removed their full-face masks and shrugged off their rebreather units.

Modeen rubbed both hands through her wet, spiky hair and glanced at Edwards. 'I'm glad we did that in daytime. Most of the dives we've done were at night and in pitch black water. It's nice to be able to see something for a change.'

'Yeah.' Edwards fixed her with a serious gaze. 'I know from what Ben's told me that the agency likes you guys to keep your night diving skills up to scratch. But you're welcome,' and he glanced at Wolf to include him, 'to come on any of the daytime recreational dives we do as part of our training exercises. We keep NatSec briefed on our training schedules, so just let Ben know you're interested and we'll take it from there.'

Modeen and Wolf nodded their thanks as a machine-like hum and metallic clanging came from behind them. They turned to see their torpedo seals emerging from the water as the launch crew worked the docking controls at the top of the ramp.

'Right.' Edwards got to his feet. 'You can hang your suits in the wet area of the change room. I'll meet you at the stairwell and take you back to the main building.'

As they climbed back in the G-wagon, Wolf threw Edwards a pleasant, 'Thanks mate.'

'Welcome. Drop ya back at the carpark?'

'Yeah, Jo and I are headin' back to the mainland for a counter lunch. Diving always gives me an appetite.' As the wagon chugged into life, he added, 'You're welcome to join us if you like?'

Edwards flicked him a rueful look. 'Wish I could,

but I've got unfinished paperwork comin' out the wazoo.' He slid the wagon to a stop beside Modeen's Aurion and got out to shake their hands. 'Seeya here tomorrow at eighteen hundred hours for the night d—'

His last words were lost in the sudden wail of sirens, as red revolving lights flashed from the corners of each building. Thrusting up a halting hand, Edwards pressed an index finger firmly into his ear and bent his head, straining to hear over the sirens. A few seconds later he straightened but kept his hand raised in front of them.

'We've been ordered to hold our position,' he rapped. 'The base is going into lock-down.'

CHAPTER SEVENTEEN

With a squeal of all-terrain tyres, a G-wagon troop carrier roared out of the basement of a building at the back of the complex. Its rear canopy was off and two troopers in full tactical webbing, armed with M4s, hung on grimly as the troop carrier raced past the group standing in the carpark. More wagons followed closely behind, similarly loaded.

The loud chop of rotors emerged above the racket of sirens and speeding vehicles, and the three watchers glanced skyward as a Tiger ARH attack helicopter appeared. Its twin Rolls Royce turbo-shaft engines thundered it up and over the base's buildings before it went nose-down, to swoop over the troop carriers racing along the entrance road. The spiralling clouds of dust following the speeding chopper coated the three observers in fine, gritty particles and they turned their heads away, coughing and shielding their eyes.

Blinking, Wolf waved away the dust and yelled at Edwards over the noise, 'Where the hell did that Tiger come from?'

'A bunker behind the admin building,' Edwards shouted back. At Wolf's questioning frown, he added, 'It's got a retractable roof.' Cupping a hand over his ear, he bent his head to listen intently to the messages issuing from his earpiece.

When he lowered his hand and looked up, Modeen stepped closer to ask, 'What's going on?'

He put his mouth close to her ear. 'A gang of bikers slipped past the boom gate after threatening the guard on the mainland. They're heading this way, up the second bridge past Rabbit Island.'

'All this,' and she indicated the flurry of military activity with a sweep of her arm, 'for some *bikers?*'

'Yep. Like I said, we're strict on security here, and any possible threat is taken very seriously.' He glanced toward where all the action was happening. 'I wouldn't like to be in their shoes. Our guys can be quite … enthusiastic.'

Wolf threw Modeen a wink. 'Looks like we might be doin' some interrogatin' after lunch.'

She twitched an eyebrow at him while asking Edwards, 'So what happens now?'

'Hang on.' Edwards held up an index finger as he pressed the earpiece more firmly into his ear. He bent his head to listen and then raised it again. 'The lads have got the culprits detained. Now they're just waiting for the constabulary to arrive.' At their puzzled frowns, he explained, 'The intruders aren't actually on our base so they're out of our jurisdiction. We'll just hold 'em and let the boys in blue handle 'em.'

After listening again he announced, 'They've got the situation under control, so give it five and then you're right to go.'

'OK. Well, thanks Edwards.' Wolf nodded at him as he and Modeen climbed into the Aurion.

As they made their way along the access road, they saw two of the G-wagons parked side-by-side in front of the boom gate. At their approach one of the drivers moved his wagon to let them pass, and as the guard raised the boom gate for them, the Tiger thundered overhead, returning to base.

Once outside the gate, they peered down the harbour road and saw another two wagons alongside five haphazardly-parked motorcycles, their riders spread-eagled in the gravel beside the road. Four uniformed soldiers stood close by with M4s trained on their prostrate, leather-jacketed captives. When one of the bikers raised himself onto an elbow to look toward the passing Aurion as though hopeful of rescue, a soldier tapped him down again with his rifle's muzzle.

'*Turkeys*,' Wolf muttered darkly. 'What were they thinkin', playin' silly buggars so close to a high-security government facility. Not thinkin' at all, I'd reckon.'

With a nod of agreement, Modeen accelerated away

from the scene and toward the bridges and the mainland.

———

'Well,' Ben said pleasantly, 'by all reports you two had quite a busy week on the island.' He regarded them from over his desk. 'And I've been advised you both performed well, even in the interrogation training, which I'll admit can be confronting.' With a measured glance at Modeen, he said drily, 'And apparently your wrist lock came in handy again. I don't think they expect anyone to retaliate quite so forcefully – it's the first time they've had an interrogator wind up injured. It's usually the person being interrogated who comes off second best.'

At her contrite expression, Ben's eyes creased at the corners. 'Just a broken finger, nothing major. And he obviously needed reminding to stay on his toes.' They shared a conspiratorial grin and then he went on. 'Wentworth reported the night dive went off without a hitch. Apparently Paul Edwards described you as "fish", which from RAN blokes is high praise.' Ben nodded at them proudly. 'Wentworth even said you're welcome to join them on a dive any time you want a refresher.'

Modeen inclined her head in acknowledgment. 'I wouldn't mind going on some more daytime rec dives.

Let's face it, you can't see much on night dives in black water.'

Ben nodded and turned to Wolf with raised eyebrows.

'Yeah, count me in.'

'Okay.' Ben leaned forward. 'Now for today, I've arranged for you to spend some time with Reece in resources. He'll brief you on your assignment in Brisbane and provide you with whatever you need. He'll also walk you through your cover stories and give you details of the ASIS contacts you'll be working with. If you need any wardrobe or gear from the props room, make sure you take it with you when you go.'

He waved a finger in Wolf's direction. 'I've spoken with your team manager and he's happy for you to join JD on the defensive driving course. Or you can skip it if you don't feel you need a refresher.' At Wolf's careless shrug and drawled, 'Don't mind havin' another go at puttin' a car up on two wheels,' Ben scanned a document on the desk in front of him. 'The course finishes … Wednesday afternoon.' He looked up again. 'So you and JD will have plenty of time to make your way to Brisbane.'

Wolf sat back and crossed his hands over his taut stomach. 'No point in me flyin' home to WA, and then havin' to come back to Queensland a few days later, so reckon I'll hang around.'

'Good.' Ben put aside the document and leaned back in his chair. 'The function you're attending is a

Mayoral dinner. It's relatively low-key, so ASIS isn't expecting terrorist or other disruptive activity. It'll be a good undercover exercise for you.' He fixed Modeen with a firm gaze. 'Some assignments involve a lot of action, while others are surveillance and nothing much else. Agents need to be able to cope with both scenarios.'

She nodded as he continued. 'You've covered a fair bit of ground now, JD, and this undercover assignment will complete your induction.' He paused and leaned back in his chair, locking his hands behind his head. 'By now you'll have an idea of what being part of this organisation involves. If you have any reservations, I'd be happy to talk them over with you?'

When she didn't reply, merely continued regarding him, he said, 'You don't have to answer now. But if you do have any second thoughts, at any time, I want you to let me know.' He lowered his arms and sat forward. 'That goes for all our agents. We don't want anyone feeling they're alone out there. You can always talk to me about anything, without fear of retribution. That goes for you too, Wolf. Understood?'

Wolf dipped his head and grinned at Modeen's, 'Roger, Corporal.'

Ben gave a satisfied nod. 'And just like in the Army, this role involves a lot of "hurry up and wait" in between assignments. Another reason it's important you take advantage of training exercises during your down-time. They'll help hone your skills and keep you active and sharp.'

When they reached Reece's cubicle in the resources unit, Modeen leaned her arms on the partition and caught his eye. 'Hey, Reece. When do you want to run us through the assignment?'

He flicked her a glance before hastily looking away, his face reddening. He shuffled the papers on his desk and stuttered, 'Oh … right. I'll just … um … get my things together and meet you … in the briefing room. Give me fifteen minutes?'

Puzzled by his awkwardness, Modeen said slowly, 'Fine. See you in fifteen.' When they were out of earshot she leaned toward Wolf and kept her voice low. 'What's wrong with Reece? He's acting weird.'

Wolf grunted and shook his head. 'Young blokes … who the hell knows.'

After calling into the kitchen to make themselves some hot drinks, they headed down to the basement briefing room and found Reece sitting at the U-shaped meeting table, a green folder laid out in front of him.

He looked up and waved them inside. 'Close the door behind you.' As they seated themselves, he launched into his spiel as though eager to get it over with. 'This assignment is basically a baby-sitting job.' Without looking at Modeen, he handed Wolf a professionally-printed invitation. Its stylish black text sat below a coat of arms on the heavy, embossed paper.

Unfolding it, Wolf read aloud, 'The Right Honourable, the Lord Mayor of Brisbane, Councillor Trevor Campbell, cordially invites Mr and Mrs Troy Ryan,' and he winked at Modeen, 'to a Mayoral dinner being held in honour of visiting British and American delegates. The Lord Mayor trusts you will join him in welcoming the delegates to the fair city of Brisbane on Saturday twenty-eighth, in the Long Room at old Customs House in Queens Street, Brisbane, commencing at seven pm for a seven-thirty dinner. Dress is black tie. RSVP to the Mayoral Secretariat.'

He glanced at Reece, who rolled his eyes and said dourly, 'The Mayor sees the early arrival of a few G20 Summit delegates as an opportunity to make a fuss and get his face on the news. The summit isn't being held 'til the end of the month, but these American and British dudes have apparently decided to spend a bit of time in Oz beforehand. ASIS doesn't regard the func-tion as high risk, so security will be low-key.'

He watched Wolf tuck the invitation into a pocket. 'We've already submitted your RSVP in the affirmative, and I've taken the liberty of booking you a two bedroom unit at the Meriton. It's just around the corner from Customs House and an easy walk along the Bris-bane Riverwalk.'

Taking a breath and staring down at the file, Reece addressed Modeen without looking at her. 'I figured you'd drive your car back to Queensland, so I haven't worried about booking any flights.' He threw her a quick, sideways glance before fixing his gaze back on the file. 'Now … as Mr and Mrs Ryan, you've been married for three years. Troy, you work for the Australian Foreign Affairs Department here in Melbourne. Now these—'

'What about me?' Modeen interjected. 'What's my profession?'

Reece consulted the file and murmured, 'Um … we've listed you as … homemaker.'

'Homemaker?' She raised a scornful brow. 'Well that's just *great*.'

Wolf's mirth bubbled through his closed lips as Reece, determined to move on, handed over two smaller folders. 'These contain more details about your backgrounds and cover stories. They also list the ASIS contacts for the function. You're to stay unobtrusive, just mingle with the delegates and only assist security if an incident arises. You're also expected to attend a pre-function briefing with the ASIS security team leader the morning of the do.' Reece closed the file and sat back. 'Right, I think that's about it. Anything else you need, just let me know.'

Modeen studied him through narrowed eyes. 'I'll need to grab an evening gown, wig and accessories from the props room.'

'Sure.' Another sideways glance. 'Just make a note of what you take.'

'Oh, and there's a nice handbag-sized pair of stainless steel Walther CCPs in the armoury.'

'Fill out the register and they're yours. The nine mil cartridges are in the glass cabinets underneath the pistol display. Take what you need.' He looked at Wolf. 'What about you?'

'I'll grab the Armani tux I wore for one of LeMar's sessions. For a monkey suit, it wasn't too constricting.' He rubbed his stubbled chin. 'And a spare Glock and shoulder holster from the armoury. I'll leave the Glock with Jo before I head back to WA.'

'Sure.' Reece pulled out a form and a pen. 'I'll make a note that you're borrowing a weapon, but you'll still need to fill out the register. Josephine can sign it back in when she returns it.' At Wolf's resigned sigh, he said defensively, 'We have to keep track of where our weaponry ends up.'

'Doesn't every piece have a NatSec chip embedded in the stock so you can track it?'

'Yeah, but it's also important the register's kept up to date.' Reece rose to his feet, saying firmly, 'For obvious reasons I won't bore you with now.'

Early Thursday morning, Modeen and Wolf finished loading the Aurion and then set off for the first ten and a half hour leg of the trip to Brisbane. After breaking the journey in Newcastle, NSW, they'd drive the remaining eight hours to the Gold Coast.

'That should get us to my apartment on Friday afternoon,' Modeen announced as they went over their itinerary a few days before. 'And from there it's only an hour to Brisbane.'

'Sounds good to me,' Wolf muttered, 'except the bit about spending eighteen and a half hours sittin' on my ass.' He threw her a teasing glance. 'And havin' to listen to Nickelback the whole time.'

'What's wrong with Nickelback? I love their music.'

'Could-a fooled me,' he quipped, earning himself a punch on the arm.

CHAPTER EIGHTEEN

Chatting, taking turns to drive, stopping for occasional breaks, and listening to music the rest of the time, saw the eleven hour first leg of the journey pass surprisingly fast for the two agents. Now on the second leg, heading from Newcastle to the Gold Coast, Modeen pulled into a rural service station off the Pacific Highway and parked the Aurion next to an amenities block shaded by a huge fig tree. They got out and stretched, appearing to move in unison, while the hot car ticked beside them.

'Coffee first? Then we'll fuel up.' At Wolf's nod, she turned and made her way inside the servo. While the attendant cranked up the espresso machine, Modeen idly gazed out the window and watched Wolf lean his back against the car. Linking his hands behind his head he closed his eyes, as though basking in the morning sun. Shortly after, another car arrived and two women sauntered past, eyeing him off. The younger of the two stumbled over her own feet, as she first gaped at him and then preened in case he looked over.

He was certainly eye-catching, the watching Modeen conceded, with his tall, muscular physique....

Heading back to the car with their drinks, she saw him take a final stretch and then bend to open the passenger door, holding it open for her. After closing it once she was in, he slipped around the vehicle to climb behind the wheel.

She held out his cup and shook her head in amazement. 'Wow.'

'What?

'Such manners! LeMar sure did a job on you.'

'Humph.' He started the car and nudged it back onto the highway. Catching sight of her sniggering into her cup, he growled, 'Couple more days of this 'n we won't have to *pretend* we're married.'

She snorted, 'Yes dear,' and they both laughed. After taking another sip of coffee, she said with something like reticence, 'So, you ever been married? For real I mean.'

'Nah.' He kept his eyes on the road. 'Don't get me wrong, I've had a few relationships, one fairly serious.' He paused before adding, 'Bein' jilted was one of the catalysts for joinin' the Army.'

'Really?'

'Yeah, 'n it turned out to be a good move. I took to military life like a duck to water, and after a couple of tours, decided to try out for the special forces. And now I'm in national security.' He flicked her a glance. 'Another line of work where long term encumbrances can be a … disadvantage.'

She nodded into her cup without speaking.

Rancour crept into his deep voice. 'I know how it feels for a young kid to lose his Dad. That's what happened to me 'n my brother, Jake. I wouldn't want it happenin' to a kid of mine.'

She blew on her coffee and considered him. 'Was your father in the military as well?'

He nodded and a charged silence descended, broken only by road noise. After a while he asked, 'What about you? Ever been tempted to tie the knot?'

'Once.' She gazed thoughtfully out the window. 'Back when I was in the regulars. Feels like an age ago now....'

'What happened?'

'Never made it past the engagement stage.' She threw him a sideways look and her tone hardened. 'You're right about encumbrances, it doesn't pay people like us to have too many, especially the flesh-'n-blood kind. I learned that the hard way.' At his questioning glance, she sighed and murmured, 'He was killed, in Timor.'

Wolf frowned and said gruffly, 'Oh … sorry to hear that.'

She gave a brisk, lets-move-on nod. 'Anyway …

how soon after you got out of the army did you join NatSec?'

He shifted in his seat, stretching his back. 'Well, when I left the force I did a stint up north in WA, on a cattle station 'bout twenty clicks outta Newman. Did a bit of roo shootin' too.' He gave a snort. 'Not particularly challenging work, 'n NatSec pays *way* better. Been with 'em about a year now.'

'Roo shooter, hey?'

'Yeah, feral camels 'n goats too. They're a problem up there as well.' His firm lips twitched. ''N every now and then we'd kill a beast and throw a coupl'a steaks on the barbie. Nothin' like a fresh slab of meat.'

She gave an amused huff and reached across to dig him in the ribs. 'Stop with the tough talk. We both know you're just a big old softy.'

'Is that right?' He tried to keep a serious expression but failed. 'I've been called many things, but never "softy" before now.' They shared a laugh and then he sobered. 'No matter what I did after leavin' school, I just didn't fit in. Started an apprenticeship as a grease monkey, which was okay for a while. Got myself a fancy car 'n a girlfriend, 'n things were goin' okay, 'til she took off with my best mate.'

A devilish grin settled on his mouth. 'After leavin' my "good old ex-friend" with a few bruises to remember me by, I decided to chuck in the apprenticeship 'n follow in the old man's footsteps. Wasn't long after I enlisted that the CO decided I had some aptitude as a sniper and encouraged me to try out for the SASR … 'n you know the rest.' He glanced over at her. 'What about you?'

She turned away, saying tightly, 'My dad was never in the military.'

They were quiet for a while and then, keeping his eyes fixed on the road, he ventured, 'For a while there I thought you 'n Gator might've … you know.'

'We might've what?'

He shifted in his seat. 'You know … gotten close there for a bit.'

She looked down at her hands and said softly, 'We were good friends, nothing more.' Her voice rose as she lifted her chin. 'For one thing, Gator was a married man with kids. I may be a lot of things, but home-wrecker isn't one of them.' She paused before going on more calmly. 'He was having all sorts of problems at home and just needed a sympathetic ear.'

Sitting straighter, she fixed Wolf with a steely gaze. 'He was a good soldier, well suited to military life. It was adjusting to civilian life that caused him problems.'

Beside her, Wolf gave a slow nod.

'Anyway,' she sighed, 'speaking of the blokes in the unit, it's a pity we don't have more time. I would've liked to have dropped in on Spooky on the way home.'

'We'll have plenty of other chances to catch up with him. And the Spook likes a dip, so we should try 'n organise one of those rec dives with him.'

She smiled. 'I like the way you think, Wolf.'

————

Striding through the door of her penthouse some hours later, Wolf gave a long whistle. 'This is your place?'

'Yep. C'mon, I'll show you the rest of it.'

Tour over, Wolf stowed his duffel in the guest room and took a shower. Emerging later, dressed in a crumpled tee shirt and blue jeans, he went looking for Modeen and found her in the kitchen. Seeing him in casual dress, his wet hair slicked back from his chiselled face, she made a mental note to ask him his age one day. She'd pegged him as being older….

When he leaned against the counter in front of her, she turned her attention to pouring their drinks. He watched, noting she'd showered and changed too, not into the usual cargo pants and tee-shirt, but in a pretty white sundress. Its soft fabric skimmed over her slender build and highlighted the honey-gold tan of her skin. His eyes wandered over her, marvelling that even the scar on her shoulder appeared satiny in the glow of the kitchen down-lights. When his gaze crept down to her smooth, shapely legs, he suddenly became aware she'd turned and caught him staring. Hastily looking away, he raked a hand through his hair and cleared his throat.

With a bemused frown, she held out two wine

glasses. 'Let's sit out on the balcony. Take these and I'll bring the nibblies.'

In the balmy afternoon light, waves glinted as they rolled onto the sandy beach, barely ruffled by the lazy sea breeze. On the road below the unit complex, convertibles cruised past with their tops down, their passengers revelling in the warm Queensland sun. On the footpath, people strolled, jogged, or walked their dogs.

After they'd set their drinks and a cheese platter on the outdoor table, Wolf pulled up a balcony chair and sat back to rest his feet on the thick glass balustrading. 'Wow, what a great view.'

'Mm hmm.'

They sat gazing at the coastal vista, sipping their wine, nibbling cheese and crackers, and chatting idly about nothing in particular. When the sun started to lose its warmth and the breeze turned cooler, Modeen sat forward. 'What do you want to do for dinner?'

'What about a counter meal? I could go a steak and a cold beer.' Wolf licked his lips. 'Is there a pub close by? I'd rather walk than drive,' he added drily. 'Spent more than enough time sittin' on my ass these past two days.'

'My "local" is up the esplanade from here and they do a great rib-eye. By the way, you're welcome to use the pool and gym while you're here, if you feel like some exercise.'

'For now a walk'll do the trick.' Wolf dropped his

feet onto the paving and slapped a hand against his thigh. 'Right, let's go. I'm hungry.'

———

After stopping briefly at a corner café the following morning, they made their way to the meeting with the ASIS field officer. They were ushered into an office where a harried-looking man sat behind an untidy desk. He glanced up at them and gave a disdainful sniff.

'You'll have to excuse me if I don't come across all warm and fuzzy,' he said curtly. 'I'm just sick to death of babysitting.'

'Babysitting….' Modeen frowned. 'I assume you're not referring to us?' When the man raised an eyebrow as if to say, 'If the shoe fits…', she had to grab hold of Wolf's arm to stop him lunging across the desk.

Seeing that, the man smirked. 'Feelin' lucky, mate? Then you should know I was a champion boxer in the Navy.'

Scorn glittered in Wolf's eyes. Turning to Modeen, he drawled, 'That explains it. Seaweed suckers never were real smart.'

She raised her hands in a placating gesture. 'Look,' and she regarded the man levelly, 'if you don't want us here, that's fine.' Getting to her feet, she added, 'I'll just let Ben know and we'll be on our way.'

The man's eyes widened, and as she reached for her mobile he exclaimed, 'Ben? Hang on … you mean Ben Logan?' He winced. 'You guys are the NatSec agents?' At her nod, he slapped his forehead with the heel of one hand and then waved it at her. 'Put the phone away … please.' He sighed. 'My apologies. I've been having to babysit local Feds trying to pass off as agents, but who are worse than useless.' He rose and extended a hand. 'Let's start over. Hi, I'm Darryl Connors.'

They shook hands and took their seats again. Opening a desk drawer, Connors took out a small plastic container and pushed it across the desk toward them. 'Comms units for this evening's function. When you arrive there, use these to contact me. I'll meet you in the foyer and escort you in.'

As Modeen opened the container and extracted two tiny earpieces, handing one to Wolf, Connors leaned back in his chair and put his arms behind his head. 'The venue is a security nightmare, with so many entries and exits it's not funny. It's good you could come, the more *capable* hands on deck the better. Luckily we're not expecting any problems. If we did, we would've made them choose a more secure venue.' Pausing, he gazed thoughtfully at Modeen. 'I didn't realise NatSec had female agents?'

She rose to her feet, accompanied by Wolf. 'Is that all we need to know for now?'

'Yeah, but—'

'Right. We'll see you tonight.' With a nod to Wolf, she strode out.

————

After checking into their tenth floor apartment at the Meriton, Modeen went to the window and gazed down at the Brisbane River. Sun glinted off the water as City Cats came and went, ferrying commuters and tourists alike, and leaving rolling waves in their wake.

She turned to Wolf. 'Reckon we should take a stroll along the riverwalk to check out Customs House?'

'Yep, and grab some lunch while we're out.'

————

Back in the apartment at eighteen-forty, Modeen put the final touches to her makeup and checked her wig was straight before heading into the lounge room. Pulling out a chair in front of a small writing table, she rested one foot on the rim and bent to adjust the strap of her low-heeled stiletto. The split in her backless burgundy gown opened further to reveal a length of smooth, shapely leg.

Emerging from his room, Wolf stopped and inhaled audibly.

'What?' She dropped her foot to the floor.

He came further into the room, shaking his head. 'You're one fine-looking woman, Mrs Ryan.' His lips tipped into a lopsided smile. 'Seems I have great taste in wives.'

She laughed. 'Thanks. And look at you in a tuxedo! Quite the dashing gent.' Stepping forward, she ran a hand over his smooth chin. 'And you even shaved.' She stood back to admire him. 'You don't scrub up too bad either, Mr Ryan.'

His grin widened as he held out an arm. 'Shall we go?'

'Just a sec.' Moving to the writing table, she opened a wooden case and took out a gleaming Walther CCP. After pulling back the slide she checked the breach and then let it click home. Picking up a full clip, she inserted it into the base of the weapon with a firm palm tap, and then reached for her silver clutch purse. She slipped the pistol and a silencer inside, and with a roguish wink at Wolf, snapped the purse closed.

In the lavish foyer of Customs House, the attendant gave their invitation a cursory glance. 'Welcome, Mr and Mrs Ryan.' He handed it back to Wolf. 'Please make your way inside, pre-dinner drinks and hors d'oeuvres will be served shortly.'

As soon as they entered the foyer, they saw Darryl Connors standing in the doorway of a small side office. He gave them a blank look and then recognition dawned.

'Good, you're here.' Ushering them into the office,

he rapped, 'I've got an agent posted in the front, one out the back, and one covering the kitchen area. The organisers expect up to two hundred attendees. There'll be the twenty-odd summit delegates, who you'll recognise by their accents and hovering minders, then the Mayor and his entourage, state and local government officials, the crème de la crème of Brisbane society, and the usual contingent of media hoping for some newsworthy scandal or tragedy to make their night.'

He gave a contemptuous sniff and then proceeded to check their earpieces were in place. 'Your designations are agents four and five. The other guys are checking in every half hour but you're undercover, so only contact me if you sniff out anything suspicious. According to the seating arrangements you're on table three.' As they turned to make their way out, he called after them, 'Lookin' good, by the way. Just drop some big names and you'll fit right in with the rest of the nobs.'

In the failing daylight, a sprightly figure in a baggy black suit climbed the lichen-green stairs leading to the terrace at the rear of Customs House. Skirting the areas lit by burning torches mounted on long poles, the young man scurried to a shadowy part of the garden, squatted on his haunches, and merged with the shadows.

A short time later he checked his watch, just as a light blue Kombi van turned into the building's side access way with a peevish squeal of tyres. As it bumped down the drive and skidded to a stop next to one of the side doors, a man in a tuxedo leapt out and bounded up the stairs to rap on the door. He stood shuffling his feet as the heavy locks were released, and then stiffened as the door was opened from within.

A tall man appeared in the doorway, wiping sweat from his florid face. His suit coat, while stylish, struggled to sit flat against his portly frame and bulged in places when he raised an agitated hand in the air. *'Finally!* Hurry up, you're late. The Mayor won't be pleased if he sees the band setting up while the VIPs are arriving.' As he turned away, the function manager muttered darkly, 'And it'll be all *my* fault, no doubt.'

Puffing, 'Sorry, car trouble,' the man from the Kombi hurried back down the steps to knock on the van's side door. It slid open, and a woman in a simple black evening gown and two more tuxedo-clad men filed out. As the first man began emptying the van of its contents, the other three grabbed violin, cello, and viola cases and hurried up the stairs, just as the young man in the baggy suit appeared from around the back of the Kombi.

'Give'ya a hand, mate?'

The flustered band leader barely glanced at the smiling young man. 'That'd be great, thanks. We're running late.' He pointed to the growing pile of gear by the van. 'Gotta get this lot inside and set up before the manager has a coronary.'

His smiling helper promptly scooped up a music stand, stool, and a bag of sheet music and skipped up the stairs. Once inside he made for the polished timber stage area, where the other string quartet members were hastily setting up. When the woman glanced over as he dumped the gear on the stage, he threw her a winning smile and announced he was going back for another load. She gave a distracted nod and went back to work, as the young man made for the door again. Along the way he kept looking over his shoulder before slipping through an opening in the timber-panelled corridor and into the growing assembly of elegant guests. Assuming a jaunty air, he meandered through the crowd to the as-yet unmanned bar, where he settled himself on an intricately carved wooden stool in a dark corner. After casting a furtive glance around, he bared his teeth in a triumphant grin and reached into a jacket pocket for his mobile phone.

His fingers were not quite steady as he typed a hasty text, and they visibly shook as he pressed SEND.

CHAPTER NINETEEN

Modeen rested a hand lightly in the crook of Wolf's firm, suit-coated arm as they mingled, sipping champagne and trying not to let their boredom with polite small talk show. Through their earpieces they heard the other agents going through their regular check-ins.

'Agent one. Front, check.'

'Two. Rear, check,'

'Three. Kitchen, check.'

Connor's gravelly voice came over the comms. 'Group leader, all clear.'

When Modeen leaned into Wolf, he bent his head to hear her whisper, 'Anything look out of place to you?'

He swept a casual glance over the room's lavish décor, softly lit by crystal chandeliers high above. In the centre of each carefully situated table, a large vase overflowed with white roses, while the surrounding chairs sported matching white linen covers, sashed with wide satin ribbons tied in bows. As the last well-dressed dignitaries swanned into the already crowded room, he noticed the flush-faced manager hovering nearby give a signal, and the quartet launched into their first tune.

Turning back to Modeen, Wolf saw her incline her head toward the bar. He immediately looked over and spotted a gangly young man lurking in one corner, head bent so his face was in shadow. Wolf peered closer, taking in the man's baggy suit, the pants above a pair of long-toed brown shoes, the shirt cuffs protruding an inch past his coat sleeves, and the unfashionably wide black tie fastened in a school boy's knot.

He heard Pierre LeMar's scandalised voice in his head. *'Non, non, non! Cette cravate*, zis knot, it is so out of place ... it is *vulgaire, oui?'*

As he watched, the young man took a surreptitious glance around the room from beneath the ragged fringe of his lank, shoulder-length hair, before once more lowering his gaze to the glowing screen of his mobile phone.

Bending to brush his lips against Modeen's cheek, Wolf murmured, 'Good spottin', sweetheart.'

His last word brought unexpected warmth to her face and she frowned inwardly. Then the smartly-dressed MC boomed from the podium, 'Ladies and gentlemen, your attention please. Proceedings are about to start, so please begin moving to your assigned seats. Thank you.'

As groups of talking, laughing guests and their minders checked the seating chart and milled around the tables, Modeen noticed the young man emerge from his gloomy corner to skulk toward the amenities.

Wolf dropped another kiss on Modeen's cheek and whispered, '"Suit boy" is all yours. I'm off to check the perimeter.' He drew back, a half smile playing on his lips. 'Try not to break him.' With a dip of his dark head, he left her side and made his way through the milling crowd to the main entrance.

Feeling a hand on her arm, Modeen turned to see the lady mayoress gazing at her with an indulgent expression.

'It's Josephine, isn't it?'

Seeing her quarry disappear down the corridor, Modeen swallowed her impatience and dipped her head in greeting. 'You have a good memory, your lady-ship,' she said sweetly. 'We were only briefly intro-duced earlier.'

The mayoress bestowed a regal smile on her and said with plum firmly in mouth, 'One does one's best.'

As Modeen nodded and made to move away, the mayoress kept hold of her arm. 'I must say, my dear, it's delightful to see a married couple so devoted to one another.'

When this was greeted with an uncertain frown, the mayoress gave a tinkling laugh. 'I'm speaking of you and your husband … Troy, isn't it?' With an imperious wave of a heavily jewelled hand, she indicated the gap in the crowd made by the departing Wolf. 'You can't have been married long, my dear?' She gave a sniff and touched a tissue to her nose. 'I say that because you're obviously still crazy about each other.' She raised a sardonic, sculptured eyebrow at Modeen, who gaped at her.

Deciding the young woman was simply overawed by her presence, the mayoress gave a delighted titter. 'It's alright, you don't have to say anything. Just take my advice and enjoy it while it lasts, my dear.' She gave a knowing wink. 'Now,' and she sighed, 'I'd best join my own husband.' With that, she patted Modeen's arm before gliding away.

Modeen stared after her, wondering if she and Wolf were going overboard with the whole married couple act, and then shook her head to clear it of thoughts other than the mission. She roused herself to hurry past the bar area, and glimpsed the young man at the end of the corridor. He was loitering outside the restrooms, trying to appear innocuous.

Hearing her approach he glanced up and stiffened, appearing undecided whether to scarper or to bluff his way out. In the end he chose the former, and ducked inside the men's toilet.

After pausing outside to consider her options, Modeen continued along the corridor to the ladies'.

She entered, leaving the door slightly ajar behind her, and waited just inside.

Wolf kept to the shadows as he left the main entrance and headed right toward the riverwalk. Pressing a finger to his earpiece he whispered, 'This is agent four. I have a dark green sedan with four occupants reversing fast down the north-east side.'

From inside the restroom Modeen heard the door of the gents bang, and peered out to see the young man scuttle past. She murmured into her earpiece, 'Agent five. Suit boy's on the move,' and broke cover to follow as he made for the north-eastern end of the building.

Listening to her report, an anxious Connors frowned. Who the hell was suit boy?

As the green sedan came to a screeching halt, four occupants sprang out and rushed to the side door of Customs House, pulling their trench coats tighter around their scruffy jeans and tee shirts. When one of their coats flapped open and he glimpsed a rifle barrel beneath its folds, Wolf bounded out of the shadows, pulling out his Glock and holding it low at his side as he sprinted toward them.

• • •

The young man's hands shook as he fumbled to unlatch the bottom bolt on the heavy side door. He sucked in a relieved breath as the bolt finally slid home. Now only the top one to go. He reached for it, hands steadier now he had success within his grasp. Just a few inches….

The blow to the back of his head made him cry out in shock and pain as his face slammed into the mahogany wall. When he stayed upright, pressed against the wall, he copped a knee to the back of the leg and crumpled in a blubbering heap to the floor.

Looking down at him, Modeen pressed her earpiece and said evenly, 'Agent five. Suit boy is down.'

As he moved to stand between the sedan and the group of four young men milling around the side door, obviously waiting to be let in, Wolf noticed the bulges of concealed weapons beneath their coats. He growled, 'Can I see your invitations?'

When as one they spun around, yanking their weapons free and pointing them at him, he raised a disdainful eyebrow and drawled, 'You get paint on this tux and there's gonna be trouble.'

They gaped at him and then one of the youths stepped forward to say in a squeaky, tremulous voice, 'Let us go and … and … you won't get hurt.'

Wolf gave an amused huff. 'Believe me, you're not going anywhere.' Raising the Glock, he reached a casual hand under his jacket and took out a silencer. After making sure they could see him fitting it to the pistol, he took a sideways glance at the car and then shot out a front and back tyre.

At the sound of the shots the youths flinched, gasped, and jumped back. Two dropped their guns on the ground and threw their hands in the air.

'Smart move.' Wolf grinned roguishly at the group. 'Now you two,' and he pointed at the youths still holding their weapons in unsteady hands, 'put down the paint guns. And all four of you, lie face down on the floor … NOW.'

As the youths did as they were told, agent two came sprinting around the corner from the rear of the building.

Putting a finger to his earpiece, Wolf announced, 'Group leader, we have four males detained outside the north-eastern side of the building, and one inside. You might want to call the police.' He turned to agent two. 'You right to watch this lot?' At the agent's nod, Wolf rapped on the side door with a large hand and called, 'Jo, it's me.'

He heard the top bolt release and then the door opened. He stepped inside to find Modeen standing over a whimpering suit boy. His arrival seemed to stir the young man to action.

Modeen watched idly as he raised his head, and when he tried to get up, she put a high-heeled foot in the centre of his back and pushed him back down. He responded by trying again. This time she shoved the heel of her shoe against the small of his back, until he cried out with pain and flattened himself against the floor.

The third agent had left his post in the kitchen to join them at the rear door. Wolf gestured for him to assist the agent watching the four youths outside, as Connors hurried over to them.

'Report.'

'Five youths looking to make some sort of statement with paint guns. One here, and the other four,' and Wolf pointed a thumb toward the side door, 'outside.'

Putting a finger to his ear Connor listened and then announced, 'Police are on their way. You two should join your table before you're missed.' He gave them an approving nod. 'We'll take it from here, thanks.'

Back at the Meriton, Wolf dropped his jacket over a chair and undid his bow tie. Flicking open the top button of his white shirt, he flopped onto the couch and spread both arms along the backrest. Modeen handed him a nightcap as she sank down beside him, after first kicking off her shoes.

He took the glass and watched as she folded her legs neatly beneath herself and settled back, asking idly, 'Where'd you get the brandy?'

'I popped into the bottle-o beside that café where

we had lunch. You were busy checking out the River Cats.'

'Oh, right.' He nudged her with an elbow. 'I thought you were shopping for shoes.' When she rolled her eyes at him, he gave a bark of laughter. 'Don't think I didn't notice you window-shopping along the riverwalk.' He wiggled his eyebrows at her and took a mouthful of the spirit, holding it on his tongue. Resting his head back against the headrest he gazed at the ceiling and sighed. 'Ya know, if it wasn't for the paint boys, this would've been a pretty boring night.'

At her quipped, 'They did add a bit of colour,' he gave an amused snort. 'Very droll.' Raising his head, he leaned closer to clink his glass against hers.

'According to the group leader,' she went on, 'they were uni students wanting to make a public protest about Australia's involvement in Iraq.'

She lifted a scornful eyebrow as Wolf grunted, 'Turkeys. What would they know about what's happenin' over there.' He took another mouthful of brandy and when he lowered his glass, found her gazing at him.

Their eyes locked and then he drained his glass and rose to his feet. 'I'm catchin' the flight to Perth tomorrow,' he said gruffly. 'When are you headin' back to the coast?'

'In the morning.' Uncurling herself, she rose, went to the window and gazed out at the city lights.

Behind her, Wolf strode to the apartment's kitchen and set his empty glass on the counter. Turning, he found his eyes drawn to her once more. As his gaze roved over her firm but womanly figure in the backless gown, and took in the satiny skin of her middle and lower back, he frowned, cleared his throat, and announced in a thick voice, 'Right. Well … see you in the morning.'

Calling, 'Night,' she turned to watch him go and then looked out at the city again. Swirling the remaining brandy in her glass and musing, *we're not in the military anymore,* she swallowed the last of the deep amber spirit in one gulp.

She moved to the kitchen and placed her empty brandy balloon next to Wolf's. For a long moment she stood staring at the two glasses, so alike, and sitting side-by-side on the counter. Turning, she padded quietly down the corridor and stopped outside the second bedroom. After a brief hesitation, she gave the door a perfunctory tap, opened it, and stepped inside. Closing the door behind her, she leaned back against it.

Wolf stood by the bed, bare to the waist, staring at his unexpected visitor.

Biting her lip, she let her eyes linger on his muscular arms and shoulders above a broad, well-defined chest and lean hips, and released a hot breath. At his questioning frown, she tilted her head and said, 'Well … we *are* married. Sort of.'

He grew very still and fixed her with an intense,

dark-eyed gaze, before saying slowly in a deep, gravelly voice, 'Works for me.'

As he moved toward her, she reached behind and turned off the lights.

———

Angelo darted forward, beaming. 'Good-a to see you back at home on-a the Gold Coast.' He showed her to her usual table. 'Alone again, ah?' With a dramatic hand-on-heart gesture, he announced, 'It-a breaks-a my heart, such a beautiful lady all-a by herself.' He gave a regretful shake of his head and pulled out a chair, indicating it with a one-armed flourish and calling, 'Gina! Some red-a wine for the Modeen-a, *grazie.*' Once Modeen was settled, he pushed her chair back in. 'You-a having your usual, yes?'

She gave a smiling nod as a plump, dark-haired lady, smelling strongly of garlic, bustled to the table holding a bottle of shiraz.

Angelo took it from her and picked up a glass. 'Now, some garlic bread and-a carbonara for our guest.'

With a quick smile at Modeen, Gina scurried to the kitchen as Angelo poured the wine, setting the glass on the table with another flourish. '*Buono!* Now I go check on your meal-a.' Bowing, he left her swirling the dark red wine in the glass, gazing at it as though contemplating its colour and aroma. In truth, her thoughts were further afield….

The sudden buzz and vibration of her NatSec mobile broke into her thoughts. With a sigh she pulled it out of a pocket and looked at the caller ID.

Unknown.

After first checking if anyone was within earshot, she touched a finger to the screen and put the phone to her ear. 'Bennet.'

A familiar deep voice said, 'Your first solo assignment. Timeline three weeks from now. Sending through the details shortly. Good luck and let me know if there's anything you need.'

There was a short buzz and the phone went dead.

Staring at the now blank screen, she clicked her tongue.

Hi Ben, good to hear from you. I'm fine, thanks for asking.

The phone chimed, announcing an incoming text. On opening it she found an event number above a photograph of a swarthy, sour-faced man. His personal details and current location were listed beneath the photo. Switching off the phone, she tucked it into a pocket and sat back to sip her wine.

Fronting up to the counter to pay the bill a while later, she was wrapped in a warm, garlicky hug as Angelo enthused, 'You come back-a soon, ah?'

· · ·

Back at her apartment, she opened her laptop and typed a residential address into the online map. The on-screen globe did a few revolutions and then zoomed in on a property in New South Wales.

Hmm ... rural acreage just outside of Katoomba, about a hundred clicks west of Sydney.

She zoomed in to highlight the main building on the property, a sprawling hacienda-style homestead.

The following morning, freshly showered after an early jog along the beach, she sat on the bed and logged in to her NatSec laptop. Opening the 0309 events file, she scrolled through the folders and opened the one titled IMAGES. After flicking through the photos of Salvatore Batista and his known associates, pausing every now and then to study them, she clicked on a close-up shot of the hacienda. It was much the same as the online map image, only more recent and more detailed.

The satellite photo showed what appeared to be two armed sentries on the homestead's roof. She gave a grim smile and, zooming in to examine the terrain surrounding the hacienda, traced a finger along the road that snaked around the property.

Crossing the basement to her NatSec Aurion, which she'd taken care to park so the car's trunk faced the wall for added privacy, she squeezed between the narrow gap and clicked the boot open. Moving with purpose, all the while keeping a cautious eye and ear to her surroundings, she transferred the Vanquish sniper rifle into a custom-made backpack which she slung over one shoulder. She then picked up the PPX, removed the clip, pulled back the slide, and checked the breach.

Clear.

After palming the clip back into place and tucking the pistol in the front waistband of her jeans, she tugged down her jumper to conceal it and then collected two extra clips and the silencer from the case. These she stuffed into a spare pocket on the backpack.

Done.

Closing the boot firmly, she returned to the apartment and stowed the PPX among her clothes in one of the GTR's panniers, along with a pair of hi-tech military binoculars and night vision goggles.

Back in the basement at o-five hundred the following morning, she loaded the panniers on the GTR while mentally calculating her ETA.

A ten hour trip.

She glanced at her watch.

Should be there around fifteen hundred hours, depending on road conditions.

After strapping the tailor-made backpack securely across the rack, she paused to once more run over the checklist in her head before donning her helmet and seating herself on the bike.

Eight hours later she turned off the M1 motorway at Wahroonga and joined the M2 at Pennant Hill, heading west toward the Blue Mountains and Nilla's Place, her bed-and-breakfast accommodation just off Bathurst Road in Katoomba.

Nice and convenient, about twenty clicks south of the target.

Arriving at the B-and-B, she checked her watch before dismounting from the warm bike.

Right on fifteen hundred hours.

After stretching and breathing deeply of the cool mountain air, she eyed the Edwardian-styled gable that would be her home for the night. The afternoon sun glinted off the fresh silver-grey and white paintwork. Neatly trimmed Jacaranda trees shaded the house's front and side verandas, and a fragrant cottage garden of roses, lavender, foxgloves and daisies edged the cobbled front path. Bees buzzed their way happily from blossom to blossom, while tiny wrens flitted among the greenery.

Untying the backpack from the bike's rear rack, Modeen slung it over a shoulder and bent to unclip the panniers. As she made her way up the path to the front door, she saw a large ginger tabby lolling in the sunlight on the front mat. At her approach, the cat stretched and got to his feet to wind himself, purring, around her legs.

She gave him a rub between the ears, and then tapped the antique door knocker against the Edwardian-styled front door. Footsteps could be heard on the floorboards within, and when the door opened, she was greeted by a woman of average height wearing a pretty floral apron and beaming a welcome. A warm waft of baking followed in her wake.

'Hello! I'm Nilla. And you must be Jo.' She stepped back, indicating for Modeen to enter. 'Welcome to my place.'

The following morning Modeen rose and went to the bedroom window. Drawing back the lace curtains, she looked out at the clear sky and felt a crispness in the air. She turned and padded into the ensuite, to emerge minutes later wearing cargo pants, a long-sleeved shirt, hiking boots, and a plain khaki jumper tied around her shoulders.

On entering the dining room, looking forward to a hearty breakfast, she found two couples sitting at sunny window tables. One of the men glanced her way as he bit into a triangle of golden buttered toast, but at his wife's sharp look, quickly returned his attention to his plate.

'Good morning.' Nilla walked up, smiling and wiping buttery hands on her apron. 'Sit anywhere you like. Are you having bacon and eggs? There's also breakfast cereals, yogurt, toast and fruit,' and she pointed to a tall antique kitchen dresser stacked with an array of jars, packets and full-to-the-brim bowls.

Modeen smiled. 'Just poached eggs with toast, and a coffee please.'

'Too easy.' Nilla scurried away, returning minutes later with a steaming mug of coffee and shortly after that, a plate loaded with triangles of buttered sourdough toast, two neatly poached eggs, and a sprig of parsley glistening with dew drops.

'From my own garden, and my own chooks,' she said proudly, placing the plate in front of her guest with a flourish. Standing back, she eyed Modeen's outfit. 'Planning some outdoor activities today?'

Modeen paused imperceptibly before replying, 'Going for a hike.'

Nilla beamed. 'Oh! Well, you've chosen the right day for it. Are you familiar with the area? There are quite a few nice walking tracks.'

Taking a sip of her coffee, Modeen replied carefully, 'I'm hoping to catch sight of some Rainbow Lorikeets and Scarlet Robins.'

'Oh yes, we have some beautiful birds around these parts. And there's a big aviary just down the street.' Nilla pointed eastward along Bathurst Road.

'That's nice, but I prefer to see them in the wild.'

Just then, another couple entered the dining room

and Nilla hastened away to greet them, saying, 'Well, have a nice day, Jo.'

Relieved to avoid further questioning by her gregarious host, Modeen gave her breakfast a businesslike eating and then quietly left the sunny room.

Outside, she donned her helmet, fired up the GTR and headed for the highway. Following the coordinates on her GPS, she pulled up on the opposite side of the hill from Batista's property. With a quick check for traffic, she circled round, gave the heavy road bike some revs to lighten the front wheel, and jumped it over the curb.

After snaking the big bike motocross-like up the dirt walking trail as far as the narrow track would allow, she parked it behind some thick foliage and killed the motor. Dismounting, she retrieved a small backpack from one of the panniers and tossed in a pair of binoculars and her Walther PPX. Then she stood back and checked the bike was hidden from all but the most determined search, before setting off on foot.

The steepness of the trail had her breathing hard when she reached the top of the hill. Resting on her haunches, she took in the sweeping vista. Perched on the foothills, surrounded by sprawling acreage and no doubt enjoying panoramic views, sat a pretentious hacienda-style homestead.

It was just as the online map had pictured it.

Taking the binoculars from her backpack, she checked the distance to the homestead using the rangefinder function, and then surveyed the terrain between herself and the building. After locking onto a concealed rocky outcrop about a quarter of the way down, she noted the distance and gave a slow nod.

That's the spot.

Next she checked for any activity at the homestead.

Pretty quiet … no vehicles visible on the semi-circular driveway … one sentinel on the roof … a couple of Rottweilers locked in a dog run.

Back in her room at Nilla's Place, having showered and changed, she took out her phone and sent Ben a quick text.

Recon completed.

0309 still a go?

Glancing at her watch and finding it was only late morning, she thought about taking a stroll before lunch. Then her phone beeped and vibrated with an incoming message.

Affirmative.

You have a green light.

CHAPTER TWENTY

The shadows lengthened and the air temperature dropped another degree, as Modeen once more jumped the curb and nosed the big bike along the path. Stopping in the same spot as that morning, she dismounted and pulled off her jumper to reveal a long-sleeved camouflage shirt. After bundling the jumper onto the GTR, she untied the custom-made backpack from the bike's rear rack and slipped the straps over her shoulders, fastening them with a firm tug.

Working swiftly, she retrieved the PPX, binoculars and night vision goggles from the panniers, screwed the silencer to the pistol and then pushed the gun through the thick khaki belt at the back of her pants. Clipping the binoculars and goggles onto the sides of the backpack, she rolled the bike into the shrubbery and set off on the uphill trek.

Along the way she came across fresh wallaby droppings and heard rustlings in the undergrowth surrounding the track, as nocturnal fauna began to stir. When she reached the summit she once more got down on her haunches to catch her breath, the dying rays of the sun barely warm against her back. Unclipping the binoculars, she peered through them at the homestead below.

All quiet.

Crouching low, she made her way downward. Where the vegetation thinned, she crawled on her belly and reached the rocky outcrop a quarter of the way down the ridge without incident. After finding a level spot behind a good-sized boulder, she paused to once more unclip the binoculars. Resting her forearms on the boulder while keeping her head low, she took a range reading to the homestead.

Eight hundred and ten metres.

She aimed the binoculars at the driveway and saw a dark-coloured Ford and an ostentatious limo – Batista's ride, probably – parked there. Lowering the binoculars, she dropped back behind the boulder and slipped the backpack to the ground. Opening it, she unpacked the sniper rifle and swiftly assembled it.

With one last check of distance to target, elevation, wind speed and direction, she adjusted the scope and gently rested the weapon on the bipod stand at her side. With a grim smile, she took out her phone.

Last chance, Batista.

She typed a quick text.

In position. Still a go?

After pressing SEND, she picked up the binoculars again. A second later the phone vibrated and she checked the screen.

Confirm you have a green light.

She exhaled.

Guess you're all out of chances, Batista.

Settling herself into a comfortable position, she checked her watch.

Eighteen thirty hours.

She put the binoculars to her eyes … and waited.

The white hacienda was an easy target, standing out boldly against its darkening surroundings. She could clearly see two sentinels on diagonal corners of the roof, armed with what looked like M4s. Scanning lower, she spotted two more guards in the front of the building and one in the rear yard.

She lowered the binoculars.

M4 Carbines … 5.56 millimetre … accurate up to five hundred metres. More close-quarter than distance weapons.

Her eyes narrowed.

Unless they get lucky with a lob, I should be safe here.

By twenty hundred hours she sat in almost total darkness, the moon lending a mere silvery tinge to the gloom. She got to her feet and stretched, before settling again to resume her watch. When she noticed a third guard step onto the homestead's roof and beckon the other two over, she grabbed the Vanquish and rested the barrel on top of the boulder, using the rifle's high-powered night scope to get a clearer view.

Oh hell, they're fitting thermal imaging scopes.

Slipping behind the boulder again, she pulled a thermal sheet from the backpack and wrapped it around the top half of her body and over her head. Then, placing the rifle in a narrow gap between the boulder and a neighbouring rock, she wriggled herself into position, lying flat on the ground behind the gun.

She took a deep breath and pulled the rifle's bolt up and back, then forward and down, guiding the first fifty cal projectile into the breach. Tugging the thermal sheet close around her head and scope in an effort to keep her heat signature as small as possible, she once more settled in to wait.

The guards began scanning the area through their thermal imaging scopes as she watched from above. When the closest guard to her position scanned up and along the ridge toward her, she held her breath and focused her rifle's cross hairs on him. She breathed out on seeing him indicate 'all clear' to the others, but her body remained rigid, on alert.

That 'all clear' will change to an alarm as soon as I fire off the first round and my rifle heats up .

She drew her head back and rolled it, releasing the tension in her shoulders.

It's too late to change tack. If I move now, they'll spot my heat signature easily. Against this rocky terrain I'll stand out like a beacon.

She eased herself into position again.

If I get a clear shot I'll take it. If not, I'll bug out in the early hours. The guards'll be less vigilant then.

At the hacienda bar, a swarthy, fat-bellied man threw a couple of ice cubes into a glass and splashed a double shot of rum over them. Opening a set of double doors, he strutted out to the pool area, a lit cigar protruding from his wet, fleshy lips.

On the hillside above, Modeen stared through the scope and murmured softly, 'Welcome home, Mr Batista.'

Steam rose from a corner of the pool as the separate spa section bubbled invitingly. As he sauntered toward it, Batista undid the tie on his robe revealing glimpses of a dark, hairy body swathed in rolls of flab.

Modeen grimaced.

On reaching the spa, he dropped the robe and stepped naked into the bubbling water.

Modeen pulled her head back and blinked.

Great. Now I have THAT image stuck in my head.

Putting her eye to the scope again, she saw Batista lean back in the spa and take out the cigar long enough to drain his glass. After biting down on the stogie again, his lips parted as a tall, leggy brunette emerged from the same double doors. Clad in a thick white bathrobe and walking with a hip-bone swagger, the brunette made her way toward Batista while he sat leering at her.

When she paused near the spa as though uncertain, he barked something at her. Modeen saw the brunette's shoulders visibly sag as she slowly dropped her robe. In contrast to his nakedness, hers was all smooth, slender lines and satiny skin. She slipped into the water opposite him, and he immediately moved in to nuzzle her neck and paw at her ample breasts. When she turned away as though repulsed, he gave a lewd sneer and snaked out a hand to grab her face. Digging fat fingers into the soft flesh of her cheeks, he yanked her face close to his again. Seeing her flinch, his sneer widened and he sat back to yell something at the building.

A minute later, a house maid scampered out carrying a tray of glasses and a bottle of champagne in an ice bucket. In her haste, the young woman tripped on the raised edging around the spa and fell forward, grabbing the rim of the spa to stop herself from face-planting on the hard paving.

Modeen winced as she watched the tray and its contents sail through the air to land in the water, where they danced briefly on the bubbles before sinking to the bottom. She imagined she could hear Batista's outraged roar as he reached out to grab a handful of the unfortunate maid's hair. Pulling the wailing young woman toward him and against the spa, he dragged her over the edge and thrust her head underwater.

She kicked out and flailed her arms, splashing water everywhere and scratching him with her fingernails as she tried desperately to break free from his cruel, vice-like hold. He threw back his head as though amused by her struggles, while beside him, the brunette's hands flew to her mouth as she looked on in horror.

Then a sharp whistle reached their ears, followed by a wet thud. Batista's body jerked violently and the maid found herself abruptly released from his grip. She clawed herself out of the spa to collapse to the paving, dripping and gasping for air.

In the spa, the brunette pressed her hands tighter against her mouth as a scream rose in her throat. Wide-eyed with shock, she watched Batista's eyes roll back in his head as he slumped sideways, a charred crimson hole above his left brow. And when his flaccid body rolled face-down in the water, revealing the shattered mess at the back of his skull, the scream burst from her, increasing in pitch as she scrambled out to fall heavily to the paving.

Behind her, the water, once perfectly clear, now bubbled red and blotchy with human tissue. As though uncaring or unaware of the grazing to her knees, she ran frantic hands over herself to remove the traces of blood, hair and brain matter deposited on her body by the spa's bubbling action.

A guard skidded to a halt beside the spa and reached down to haul his boss's body above water. When Batista's shattered head appeared, the guard gave a violent jerk and dropped him again. Stepping back, he took in the crimson streak on the spa wall where Batista had been sitting and the splatter on the paving behind. Whirling around, he scanned the hillside and levelled his assault rifle. As he fired randomly upward into the darkness, the brunette grabbed her robe, helped the sobbing maid to her feet, and together they ran for cover.

On the near edge of the roof above, the sentinels had taken up positions behind a metre-high wall. It provided cover and a handy resting platform for their rifles. They peered through their thermal imaging scopes, scanning the hillside as all the homestead's outdoor lights blazed on. The guards from the front yard emerged through a gate, one of them straining to keep two leashed Rottweilers in check.

As bullets ricocheted off the terrain below her, Modeen stayed low, watching through her rifle's scope. She saw the guard in the rear yard release the two slavering Rottweilers, who bounded forward and out of sight. One of the guards on the roof pointed toward her position and began lobbing bullets, trying to zero in on her, as the other guard joined him. Bullets rained down within metres of her, only to cease when she squeezed off another two rounds.

As both guards on the roof jerked and fell backward, she saw the three remaining guards follow the Rottweilers into the scrub and disappear into the darkness below her. Moving swiftly, she dismantled the Vanquish and stowed it in the backpack. Slinging the pack over one shoulder, she took a few seconds to collect the spent cartridges from the ground before donning her night vision goggles. As she began the hill climb she reached around to yank the PPX from her belt.

At the summit, she paused to listen and her ears caught a harsh barking in the distance. She picked up the pace, staying low and hurdling obstructions as she jogged down the track. After squeezing through a narrow section of the trail lined with boulders and heavy foliage, she stopped again. The dogs sounded louder and closer now, and there was still around a hundred metres between her and the GTR.

I'm not gonna make it.

Positioning herself five metres from the narrow pathway, she pulled back and released the slide on the PPX, slamming the first round into the chamber. The dogs were very close now, she could hear them pounding toward her along the trail, grunting wetly as they ran. She unscrewed the silencer from the PPX and got down on her right knee. Resting her left elbow on her bent thigh and using that hand to support her right arm, she sighted down the pistol's barrel as the first dog bounded into view.

Seeing her, it snarled and accelerated, the moonlight glinting off the saliva dripping greasily from its jowls. The sound of the PPX was deafening as she fired two quick rounds, blasting off chunks of rock from directly in front of the dog. It gave a yelp, skidded to a stop, and then darted sideways into the thick undergrowth.

The second dog was made of sterner stuff. It continued to charge at her, lips drawn back over a fearsome set of teeth, the glint of the hunt in its eyes.

Modeen released two more rounds.

The fanged black assassin yelped and stumbled, before pitching muzzle-first to the dirt and sliding to a stop at her feet.

Rising swiftly, she sprinted down the path to the GTR, shrugging off the backpack as she ran. As soon as she reached the bike, she stowed the binoculars in the panniers, tossed her night vision goggles onto the seat, and shoved the PPX in the side pocket of her camouflage pants. Pulling on her jumper, she slipped the backpack over her shoulders, donned the goggles again, and reversed the big bike from its hiding place.

She paused for a second to listen....

No sound of pursuit.

The men couldn't move through the foliage as quickly as the dogs had.

She pushed the bike down the slope and got on as it coasted along the winding path. When it lost momentum she fired up the big motor and roared off down the trail. On nearing the highway, she stopped to switch on the headlights and remove her night vision goggles. Bumping the GTR over the curb, she leaned it sharply to the right and powered up the highway. After a quick glance down at the speedo, she backed off the throttle. It would do no good to attract attention to herself by flying into Katoomba at break-neck speed.

On arrival at the B-and-B, she parked behind the house, unclipped the panniers, and made her way quietly to her room. After dumping her gear on the floor, she sat on the foot of the bed, took out her phone, and typed a quick text.

Assignment 0309 completed.

After pressing SEND, she lay back on the mattress.

That could've gone better… and worse, I guess.

She stared pensively at the ceiling and then sighed and sat upright.

Time to shower and change.

As she rose to her feet, her phone vibrated with an incoming message.

Acknowledged.

Debrief o-ten hundred Monday.

The early sun's rays shone weakly, casting the barest of shadows behind the two men. They stood breathing hard from the hill climb, staring down at a dead Rottweiler.

Nudging the dog's body with a foot, one of the men

muttered, 'Said those M4s weren't adequate, they don't have the range.'

The other man gave a sarcastic grunt. 'Yeah, but the boss was never gonna take the advice of a powder monkey on that.' His lips twisted into a smirk.

'And look how *well* that worked out for 'im, mate.' His caustic retort earned the first man a sharp glance.

After taking a drag on his cigarette and lifting his chin to blow smoke into the air, the second man muttered darkly, 'Batista only hired you for your explosives expertise, *mate*.' He took another drag, coughed, and spat on the ground. 'Don't worry, I plan to keep you on.'

'Oh yeah? So you calling the shots now?'

'Dead right.' The man stuck out his chest. 'Which makes you *my* powder monkey.'

Ignoring him, the first man moved further up the track and squatted on his haunches to stare at the ground. 'From the size of these tyre tracks, it looks like our sniper was on a big road bike.'

The other man spat again. 'He's long gone now. Any idea who he might've been working for?'

The man beside him narrowed his eyes, rubbed a hand over his unshaven chin and mumbled, 'He … or she.'

CHAPTER TWENTY-ONE

odeen made her way across the tarmac, blending well with other holiday-makers in her blue jeans, tee shirt and cropped denim jacket. Inside the arrivals lounge of Melbourne's Tullamarine Airport, she saw Harper wave at her from the back of the crowd and strode over to join her.

'Hey Harper.'

'Hey Jo.'

'Thanks for meeting me.'

'No probs. C'mon, the car's on level two.'

As they made their way to a black Aurion Modeen enquired, 'The agency lets you use these vehicles for general duties?'

Harper glanced at her as the car's doors unlocked with a dull thud. 'Oh, you mean the gear in the boot?'

Modeen nodded as they both climbed in.

'I can't open it, the boot I mean.' Harper put the

Aurion in gear and nosed out of the parking bay, adding, 'I don't have that level of access.' At Modeen's inquisitive frown, she went on. 'That little device James injected into your arm is more than just a fob, ID and tracker. It's also linked to the remote on your car keys.' She grinned. 'So don't loose 'em – your keys, or your arm! Or else you won't be able to access your car's boot either.'

She flicked Modeen a glance. 'And don't be thinking you could break into it. They've made the boots on agent vehicles basically bombproof. James is the only one of us, apart from the Ops Manager, who can program them.' She gave a wry huff. 'Ironically, James is also the only one of us general staff employees *not* allowed to use the vehicles.'

'Makes sense I guess.' Modeen glanced out the window at the tightening clusters of skyscrapers and congested inner-city traffic, her thoughts already far away.

On level one of the NatSec building, the two women identified themselves in the usual manner and then Harper fronted up to the scanner. Removing the belt from her dress, she dropped it into a tray muttering, 'That buckle always sets off the damn alarms.'

She headed through the revolving doors as behind her, Modeen took off her diver's watch, tugged a brown leather wallet from the back of her jeans, and placed them in a tray. Then she went through to join Harper, who was already snapping her belt back on.

Glancing at Modeen, she said wryly, 'Last time I forgot to take this off, the revolving doors locked in place so fast I almost broke my nose on the glass.'

'Yeah? Well, thanks for the heads-up.'

They shared a grin and made their way to the elevator.

Harper stepped into the lift and pressed the button for the second floor. 'Ben said to meet him in his office when you're ready.'

'Thanks.' The doors swished open moments later and Modeen strode out with a wave at Harper, who continued to the basement. After a brief stop at the staff kitchen to make herself a coffee, Modeen headed to Ben's office.

His deep voice called, 'Come,' in response to her knock. Busy flicking through a red file marked *Special Ops Event 0309*, he didn't look up when she entered the office but said pleasantly, 'Take a seat, JD.' Closing the file, he watched her pull out a chair and then leaned forward to extend a large hand. 'Congratulations on successfully completing your first solo mission.'

They shook hands and then he picked up the red file. 'Most of the time these debriefs are accomplished by videoconference or phone call, but as this was your first major assignment ...,' and he set the file down on the desk again, '... I wanted to see you in person. It gives us an opportunity to compare notes on your performance, as a learning exercise.' Sitting back, he clasped his hands over his flat stomach. 'So, tell me how you went.'

Modeen stared at him as though trying to read his mind. When he gazed levelly back at her, she sighed. 'Well … in hindsight … I could've planned it better, 'specially in light of how things turned out.'

'I assume you're referring to the additional casualties?' At her nod, he opened the file. 'This being your first solo mission, I thought it best to give you all the information we had to hand but let you plan the strategy without too much interference.' He flicked her a narrow-eyed glance. 'I'm not one for micro-managing my troops, as you know.' Lowering his eyes again to scan a page, he said matter-of-factly, 'I've read your report. Your strategy was solid, in fact I'm pretty sure that's how I would've approached the mission myself.

'You completed your assigned task without drawing undue attention to yourself or the agency, something of an achievement for a new operative.' While speaking, he flicked over the page and took a quick scan of the contents. 'The assignment was relatively straightforward and there were a number of ways you could've gone about it. Given your military background, I understand the reasoning behind your strategy.'

He raised his eyes to meet hers. 'New recruits enjoy success when they stick with what they know and are good at … initially. They soon learn that as national security operatives they have more methods – *covert methods* – at their disposal.'

She gave a slow dip of her head in concurrence.

'You read the brief on Batista?'

She nodded again.

'So from that you were aware he was a known womaniser. This may have led you to consider a different approach, like getting close enough to him to administer a lethal injection. As you discovered at Swan Island, there are many innocent-looking weapons created for just such a purpose.'

Pausing, he eyed her kindly. 'Look, JD, the agency's expectations differ from the military's, and it can take time for soldiers like us to get our heads around those differences. One of the things I want you to take from this discussion is that you're handling the transition, and performing, well.' He glanced down at the file again. 'That said, I have a few pointers for you.'

Modeen leaned forward in her chair.

'Point one – and this is the most important – never use your own vehicle or equipment when on assignment. It can be traced back to you, and if that happens you'll be exposing yourself, your colleagues, family, and friends to risk. Just call me, Leanne or Reece if you need to use a particular vehicle or weapon for a mission. We'll supply you with whatever you need and make sure it's all untraceable. Clear?'

'Clear.'

'Point two, using a bike to get off the highway and

up the hillside was a good idea, but we could've supplied you with a kitted-out trail bike, one set up for stealth. It would've got you closer to the target and given you a safer, quieter and faster egress. In addition to this, we would've had a truck waiting on the outskirts of Katoomba you could've driven the bike straight into.' He eyed her firmly. 'That's the kind of support you can, and should, call upon. Clear?'

'Clear.'

'Point three, which is *not* a direct criticism, more something to consider.' He made a tent with his fingers and gazed at her over them. 'This was a mission with one target identified for termination. The fact we ended up with multiple fatalities requires significant explanation and justification.'

At the question in his eyes, she said slowly, 'As outlined in my report, I wasn't expecting the guards to have thermal scopes. This enabled them to make my position and pin me down by lobbing their shots. With bullets raining down around me, I had to make a judgement call. I couldn't retreat and I couldn't stay there. They'd released dogs, and I knew they wouldn't take long to find me. I had no other option but to take out the two guards with the thermal scopes, not only to save my own skin but to protect the secrecy of the mission.'

He stared at her thoughtfully before saying, 'Fair enough. However, when planning missions there's another complication you need to keep in mind. In some cases, there will be informants or undercover agents on site.' When her eyes widened and she opened her mouth to speak, he raised a hand. 'In this case the two guards you took out were known criminals.'

She exhaled loudly through pursed lips.

'Of course,' Ben went on, 'you'll be made aware of any onsite assets during your mission briefings, but we can't always be in control of every situation. Ultimately, it's up to the agent on the ground to be aware of and assess all possible risks, and make the best judgement call possible. And in every case, it's imperative we do everything within our power to limit the number of casualties.'

She gazed steadily at him. 'Points taken. And I appreciate the honest feedback, Ben.'

'You did well, JD. I trust your judgement and will back you one hundred percent.' He sat forward. 'But like I said, this is different to being in the military. Here, you have more available resources and less rigidity about how you carry out missions. Naturally you're still accountable for your actions, and have to be able to justify all outcomes.'

His expression hardened. 'It's easy for some *boffin* behind a desk to criticise a mission in hindsight, I know, but we should be used to it after being in the military.' He sighed. 'Nothing got me more wild than having some weedy little pen-pushing prick tell me what I *should've* done on a mission.' He ran an agitated hand over his dark hair. 'I'd like to see how *they'd* perform under fire, running through a swamp carrying an injured mate and dodging bullets.' Taking a breath, he went on more calmly. 'I'm not about to criticise a member of my team for actions taken under duress, unless I'm absolutely certain that criticism is deserved. In this business, there'll be unavoidable collateral damage at times. Sadly, that's the nature of the beast.'

Closing the file with a snap, Ben announced, 'That's it for the debrief, unless you have any questions or something to add?' When she shook her head, he smiled at her with his eyes. 'Wanna grab a coffee? I've had enough of sitting behind this desk.'

At Modeen's greeting as she and Ben entered the kitchen, Leanne glanced over. 'Hey, Jo. You here for the week?'

'No, just the day. Heading back to the Goldy this 'arvo.'

'That's gotta be tough,' a grinning Reece butted in, 'living in Surfers Paradise. I've heard they've got the best beaches up there.'

Pleased to find him acting normally toward her again, Modeen said amiably, 'They're alright, but when you're talking beaches and waves, I reckon you can't go past Redgate or Margaret River in WA. The water there—' She was interrupted by the strident chiming of her private mobile. 'Sorry.' Taking it out, she looked at the caller ID and then glanced at the others. Mouthing, 'It's Mum,' she moved away to a corner of the room.

'Hi Mum … no, I'm in Melbourne.' She paused to listen. 'Yeah, I know about the G20 summit being held in Brisbane.' Nodding, she listened again. 'Dad's going to be there while it's on? How come?'

This time the reply took longer.

'So … he left yesterday?' She frowned. 'Oh. Okay, yes. Look, I'll be home tomorrow.' After another long pause, she bent her head and sighed. 'He's probably just busy catching up with old friends. I'm sure everything's fine. Look, I'll ring you tomorrow.'

Taking the phone from her ear, Modeen tapped the END CALL button and looked up. 'Hey, where'd Ben go?'

'Got a text message and took off, looking all serious.' Reece gave an offhanded shrug. 'Happens a lot, you'll get used to it. Usually means he's gone for a powwow with Jack or is heading over to Swan Island to meet with ASIO. Either way, it's safe to assume he's gone for the day.' He drained his mug. 'Oh yeah, and he's organised Harper to take you to the airport whenever you're ready.'

———

Her flight to Coolangatta Airport arrived on time at eighteen fifty-five. After catching a cab to her apartment, she took a shower and then poured herself a tall soda water with a squeeze of lime juice. She took a mouthful of the refreshing drink and picked up her private mobile from off the coffee table where she'd flicked it. Taking it off flight mode, she lobbed it onto the sofa.

It immediately began vibrating as twelve messages flashed onto the screen, one after the other. She frowned at them and sighed, before dialling her mother's number.

'Mum? I just got h—'

On the other end of the call Freda gasped, *'Josephine!* Where have you *been?* I've been *beside* myself!'

At the shrill note of panic in her mother's voice, Modeen stiffened but said evenly, 'Mum, calm down and tell me what's wrong.'

'It's your father,' Freda sobbed, 'he … he's been *taken!'*

# # #

If you've enjoyed this first instalment in the JO MODEEN series, please consider posting a review on your retailer's site. And I hope you'll continue sharing Modeen's adventures in the next books in the series.

FHJ

FROM NATSEC FILES

Name: Josephine Dakota MODEEN, known as "Modeen", "Jo", or "JD"

NatSec Alias: Josephine BENNET

Parents: John and Freda MODEEN

Spouse: Nil

Children: Nil

Siblings: Nil

Age: 28

DOB: 09/05/1986

Height: 5'11"

Hair: Platinum blonde, cropped short

Eyes: China blue

Character: Tough, clever, street-smart, courageous and decisive; has quick reflexes; can appear cool and aloof

Appearance: Tall, athletic, dresses boyishly but can be ultra-feminine when she chooses; has a strong but pretty face with fine features; normally wears a serious, self-possessed expression; has a scar on one cheek from a glancing bullet, and a deep scar on her left shoulder from a bullet that passed through the soft tissue

Private transport: Midnight blue Kawasaki GTR 1400cc motorbike

Weapon/s of choice: Walther PPX .9mm (referred to as "Walt")

Jobs: Soldier Regular Army; SASR specialist signaller and recipient

of Medal of Gallantry and various service medals; Security Guard;
NatSec Agent – Beta Team

Status: active

———

Name: Benjamin LOGAN, known as Ben

NatSec Alias: Ben SMITH

Parents: Garth and Marie LOGAN

Spouse: Emily Cherie LOGAN

Children: Daughter, Chelsea Marie LOGAN

Siblings: Anne-Marie WRIGHT

Age: 36

DOB: 01/11/1978

Height: 6'4"

Hair: Dark brown, short military cut

Eyes: Deep brown

Character: Strong, smart, and commanding in stature, voice,
expressions and actions; has a pleasant but business-like
disposition; is genuine, loyal, decisive and not easily flustered

Appearance: Tall with chiselled features; deeply tanned and
impressively muscular; broad-shouldered with heavily tattooed
arms; has an imposing presence

Private transport: Lexus LS600H sedan

Weapon/s of choice: Glock 17, hand-to-hand combat

Jobs: Soldier Regular Army; SASR Corporal and recipient of
Victoria Cross, Medal of Gallantry and various service medals;

NatSec Agent; NatSec Beta Team Leader based in Melbourne
VIC

Status: active

––––––––

Name: Troy WOLVERTON, known as "Wolf"

NatSec Alias: Troy RYAN

Parents: Robert (deceased) and Sophie Wolverton

Spouse: Nil

Children: Nil

Siblings: Brother Jake WOLVERTON

Age: 31

DOB: 18/08/1983

Height: 6'1"

Hair: Brown, thick and unruly in a 'who cares' style

Eyes: Dark brown, almost black, thickly lashed

Character: Strong, smart, hard-hitting and gruff; likes to keep to
himself; quick to react and slow to trust, loyal and dependable
toward those closest to him

Appearance: Dark, grizzled, strikes others as being a rough-nut;
brawny, usually unshaven, handsome despite a crooked-set nose;
muscular, scarred torso

Private transport: V8 Jeep Wrangler Renegade

Weapon/s of choice: Nemesis Arms Vanquish sniper rifle (varies
depending on situation), throwing knife

Jobs: Soldier Regular Army; SASR specialist sniper and recipient of various service medals; NatSec Agent – Delta team based in Fremantle WA

Status: active

––––––––––

Name: Luke JACKSON, known as "Spooky"

NatSec Alias: Luke WILLIAMS

Parents: Martin and Mary JACKSON

Spouse: Nil

Children: Nil

Siblings: Nil

Age: 29

DOB: 13/02/1985

Height: 5'8"

Hair: Auburn, step-cut with straight-up fringe

Eyes: Blue

Character: Softly spoken with a friendly manner and ready laugh, but a capable and tenacious soldier beneath the easy-going, stylish exterior

Appearance: Athletic, spare and wiry; has a sense of style but also a hint of steely purpose beneath the smooth veneer; has knife wound scars on his arms

Private transport: Late model Yellow Camaro ZL1 6.2L supercharged V8

Weapon/s of choice: Glock 17, MP5 assault rifle

Jobs: Soldier Regular Army; SASR point man, tracker and stealth specialist; recipient of various service medals; NatSec Agent – Beta team based in Canberra, ACT

Status: active

———

Name: Barry William PRITCHARD, known as "Bugs"

NatSec Alias: Barry PETERSON

Parents: George and Thelma PRITCHARD

Spouse: Robyn Anne PRITCHARD (divorced)

Children: Son, Cameron George PRITCHARD

Siblings: Brother Aaron PRITCHARD, sister Jane PRITCHARD

Age: 33

DOB: 18/03/1981

Height: 6'2"

Hair: Strawberry blonde, razored flat-top

Eyes: Murky blue

Character: An easy-going larrikin on the surface, but street-smart and uncompromisingly tough underneath; calls a spade a spade

Appearance: Tall, athletic, with a wide, toothy smile

Private transport: Restoring a Ford XY 351 GT Shaker

Weapon/s of choice: Mark XIX Desert Eagle .50 Action Express handgun

Jobs: Soldier Regular Army; SASR specialist medic and recipient of various service medals; NatSec Agent – Beta team, Middle East

Status: active

\- ARCHIVED FILE -
Potential Operative

Candidate Name: Eric John CROCKMAN, known as "Gator"

NatSec Alias: N/A

Parents: Paul and Janet CROCKMAN

Spouse: Denise Lee CROCKMAN (separated)

Children: Sons, Eric Jnr and Stephen CROCKMAN

Siblings: Sister, Grace Ava HARRISON

Age: 36

DOB: 20/07/1978

Height: 6'2"

Hair: Wavy black, cropped short

Eyes: Chocolate brown, hooded

Character: Intelligent, brooding; a silent type whose waters run deep; plays his cards close to his chest

Appearance: Wide at the shoulder, slim at the hip; no facial scars, bullet graze on one shoulder

Private transport: Late model Holden Commodore

Weapon/s of choice: M4 Carbine assault rifle, Glock 17

Jobs: Soldier Regular Army; SASR explosives specialist and recipient of various service medals

Status: MIA (missing in action) from the ADF

File Closed

THE NEXT BOOKS IN THE SERIES

THE MODEEN TRANSFORMATION

The 2nd action-filled Modeen adventure

Australian security agencies are on alert in the lead-up to the 2014 international G20 Summit being held in Brisbane, Queensland. Although aware of an increase in web activity on the summit site and into the backgrounds of its attending diplomats, even NatSec intel can't know what the terrorist group known as 'The Spear of Allah' is planning.
Something ex-SASR soldier and now NatSec agent, Jo Modeen, is about to find out in a very personal way....

MODEEN: BLACK OPS

The 3rd thrilling Modeen adventure

Something's not right about NatSec agent Jo Modeen's latest mission, but how can she question orders from Beta team leader Ben Logan, a man she trusted with her life in the past and wouldn't hesitate to do so again?
She must decide whether to follow her orders, or her instincts….
Realising their activities must be black ops even from NatSec, Modeen's team disperses under deep cover to unravel the web of secrets surrounding the mission, which takes them from country Victoria to Australia's national capital, and across the ocean to Kabul in Afghanistan.

MODEEN ROGUE

The 5th Modeen high-octane thriller

Decorated ex-special forces soldier and now national security agent Josephine Dakota Modeen struggles to come to terms with the fate of close teammate Troy 'Wolf' Wolverton. Critically injured during the team's most recent mission, he lies comatose in Brisbane Hospital's intensive care unit.
And the prognosis for his recovery isn't good.
Driven to pursue the organisation responsible, Modeen embarks on an unauthorised campaign of retribution.
A campaign that is both personal and perilous.

MODEEN: RULES OF ENGAGEMENT

The 7th thrilling instalment

Modeen and other members of her old squad find themselves defending honour and truth, after being subpoenaed to provide statements to a military inquiry into allegations of war crimes.

Did Ben and his Special Forces squad blatantly breach the ADF's Rules of Engagement while on deployment, or is something more sinister afoot?

MODEEN: FLASHPOINT

The 8th explosive adventure

When an LNG tanker is sunk in the Philippine Sea north of Papua New Guinea, the spotlight falls on the lucrative liquefied natural gas market. Believing an international cartel to be responsible, and that Australia's LNG plants could be at risk, the CIA tasks NatSec with gathering on-site intel.

Modeen's team is deployed to discover the saboteurs' identities, determine their next target, and find out just how far they will go....

Book one *The Modeen Factor,* introduces decorated Australian Special Forces soldier Josephine Modeen, the kick-ass heroine we'd all like to have on our side. After leaving the military, Modeen is recruited by her old CO, now a team leader with national security agency NatSec.

Book two *The Modeen Transformation,* and book three *Modeen Black Ops,* take us along on car chases, hostage rescues, and battles with terrorists, where Modeen's mantra is always the same … go hard or go home.

Available as an ebook from your favourite online retailer.

THE JO MODEEN BOX SET: BOOKS 7-9

For release 1 January 2021

In *Modeen: Rules of Engagement,* Modeen and team find themselves defending honour and truth … and Ben's past actions.

In *Modeen: Flashpoint,* the sinking of an LNG tanker north of Papua New Guinea sees Modeen and team deployed to determine what - or who - will be the next target.

In *Modeen: Strikeforce,* British SAS and US Night Stalkers are deployed to Afghanistan to rescue pilots captured by the ruthless Red Group. It's an impressive strikeforce, but will it be enough?

Pre-order now from your favourite online retailer.